NARCO

NARCO.

A NOVEL BY

EVERARDO TORREZ

Arte Público Press
Houston, Texas

This volume is made possible through grants from the City of Houston through The Cultural Arts Council of Houston, Harris County.

Recovering the past, creating the future

Arte Público Press
University of Houston
452 Cullen Performance Hall
Houston, Texas 77204-2004

Cover art "3:00 A.M.," 2000 by Miguel Ángel Reyes
Cover design by Phyllis Gillentine

Torrez, Everardo.
    Narco / by Everardo Torrez.
      p. cm.
    ISBN 1-55885-416-9
    1. Mexican American Border Region—Fiction.
    2. Drug traffic—Fiction. I. Title.
    PS3620.O64N37 2003
    813'.6—dc22   2003060267
                                     CIP

♾ The paper used in this publication meets the requirements of the American National Standard for Information Sciences—Permanence of Paper for Printed Library Materials, ANSI Z39.48-1984.

3 4 5 6 7 8 9 0 1 2   10 9 8 7 6 5 4 3 2 1

This book is dedicated to the memory of
Pablo Matías Muñoz-Molina

Smuggler's Lament

Nando Flores had never wanted a beer more desperately in his life. Even as the city plunged into the chokehold of darkness, the temperature had not slackened below ninety, yet it was still a relief from the infernal three-digit onslaught that had baked the city earlier that afternoon. He could feel the brooding storm, taste its metallic rage as he waited next to the freight elevator of the warehouse in the dark alley that stank of desolation and murder. Yes, a beer would be the shit. And as the stabs of lightning flickered in the horizon, his thoughts trailed back to the night before, to the complimentary pee-warm bottle of Carta Blanca, when he had been summoned by Mexicali Rose.

El Loro was crammed with the sweat-drenched, gyrating bodies of five hundred college students from Texas and the rest of the southwestern United States. He smiled in astonishment as he watched the orgy—the future administrators, diplomats, and legislators of that great big brother of a country within spitting distance of where he sat. What a waste, he thought as he sipped the Carta Blanca that smelled faintly like the fungus-smattered trough at the back of the club that served as the men's pisser.

"Light me, José?" lilted a voice.

He turned and saw a gleaming, jovial mouth balancing a fat cigar. Nando spun the boy his lighter. He couldn't have been more than sixteen, his blond hair stuffed frantically into his Texas A&M baseball cap with tufts and strands spilling out on all sides. There was a crusted maroon stain on the front of his Tommy Hilfiger polo shirt, and he could smell the alcohol fuming through the kid's pores as he leaned in to feed the tip of the cigar to the lighter's flame.

They were all there that night, reenacting a weekend ritual: the fraternity brothers with their earrings and sweatshirts and cologne that smelled like skunk, the girls with their pierced navels and perfect smiles and grape-sized nipples, the pimply, tequila-guzzling jocks with their crew cuts and barbed wire tattooed around their juiced biceps. His country had become a playground for the privileged gringo kids and their vices. They could get it all here—booze, narcotics, freak sex—all for a few crumpled bills, tip money that, given the exchange rate, still amounted to more than either he or his thirty million compatriots would see for a month's work.

A few months back, one of them, a doctor's son from one of the colleges on the other side, had disappeared after a spring-break excursion to one of the border cities farther east. Matamoros? Piedras Negras? He couldn't remember. After an intense search by officials on both sides of the border, his cooked bones, along with those of eight other individuals, had been excavated from a mass grave on a large chicken farm.

He could still remember the uproar caused when an intoxicated coed had been gang raped, supposedly by a band of drugged Mexican street thugs. The northern papers had denounced the *primitive morals of an erstwhile progressive nation on the verge of economic and social resurgence, a reality that would forever remain the idealistic fancy of the intellectually inclined due, in large part, to the depraved infidels who roamed the streets among the good people of Juárez, preying on the hapless, the unsuspecting.* Or some bullshit to that effect. He had cut out the article and plastered it to the dashboard of his Cougar just to remind himself why he had sworn never to cross over. Yet there had been no headlines, no breaking news coverage, no scathing editorials, no retractions when the girl finally revealed the identities of the actual rapists, two members of her college's pep band.

But they continued to come in droves, drawn by the illusions of this sin carnival, this perverted Disneyland, undaunted by the predators and parasites lurking in the cracks and alleyways of the city. And they would always come. He knew they would—and who could blame them?—as long as they had their ATM cards and hungered for the forbidden urges their self-righteous laws would not allow, and as long as there were individuals like Mexicali Rose to feed that hunger.

"How much are those wheel hounds letting you jack these days?" the oily, mackerel-faced nightclub owner asked from behind a pair of grotesquely large sunglasses that straddled her chafed, swollen nose. Two bodyguards, beefy pretty boys who undoubtedly pulled double duties indulging the sea creature's taste for filth, guarded the recesses of the room like gargoyles.

"No complaints," he answered, trying to sound as serene and expectant as possible. The preamble to a typical solicitation, he figured. The old whore queen probably wanted one of the new Jettas for one of her boy toys. Maybe. With a woman like Mexicali Rose, who dabbled in practically every swindle in town—smuggling *pollos* into the United States, aside from her nightclubs and meth labs, was her favorite venture—there was no telling, and it was this that bothered him the most about doing business with her. He hated the ambiguity, hated the edge it chiseled out of him, a surefire way of doing bad business. It was said that she was not trusted even by her own shadow.

"Finally decided to get out of the chicken coop, eh? It's

too bad. We might have been able to do some business."

"I didn't like being a slave trader," sounded Nando, his dislike for the sweating, obese shark before him increasing with every huff of carbon dioxide she heaved his way.

"It's our duty," preached Mexicali Rose, "to provide the less fortunate the possibility for a better life, no?"

"Look, I told you I don't do that anymore. If you brought me here to do that kind of business, you are wasting both our time."

"Easy, *compadre*. I wanted this meeting to be an amicable one. You want another beer, a swig of Añejo, a four-way with three *rucas* who can suck the mystery out of tomorrow?"

"You've already been too generous."

He could feel the woman studying him from behind those ridiculously large sunglasses, prodding him. The ruckus of the club had swelled to a muffled, suffocating quake of bass and bad amps, and it felt like it would all of a sudden come crashing through the cinderblock walls.

"I want your advice," she finally said. "I've been thinking about getting one of those sporty utility vehicles like all the computer executives from the north are driving these days."

"You'd better have some solid cover. Even if I could get something that big across, it would get marked the first day you drove it," explained Nando, a bit confident now. "Anything newer than a ninety-two is bad news, and certainly something that . . . obvious. . . . A two-door with the least amount of shimmer is your best bet. No chrome twenties or tinted windows or Bose system."

"Why would I want to drive a piece of shit like that?" she smirked, and then the room was drowned with the thrush of her gravelly laughter and the smarmy cackles of her two minions. "So how much you pulling in on a run these days?" she said after composing herself.

"Not much," he said, certain that she knew exactly

how much he made. "After the broker and the supplier get their cuts and I compensate for what the leeches suck out of me, I pull in two hundred, maybe three. I get by."

"You ever get tired of just getting by?"

Nando could taste the deception in her phlegmy voice as surely as if the sweaty, obese, insult of a woman was tongue-kissing him, her base quintessential being, her core, the one underneath all that expensive clothing and jewelry, spilling out all over him like an overflowing toilet. "What if you could make enough money to leave all the bullshit and slip away to one of the villages down south, find a good, clean *indita* to fuck every night for the rest of your life?"

"I wish," he finally said, wrestling with that small, unjaded segment of his brain that had, on more than one occasion, saved his ass, the one that was sending mega-decibel impulses to every fiber of his body, all of them reverberating in unison *get the fuck out of here!* But of course he couldn't, not if he ever wanted to work in Juárez again.

The first drops of rain began to drool on his windshield, their translucent etchings swabbing the interior of the car with obscure, languid shadows. He cracked the window and heard the soft rumble of the coming storm, but nothing more. ZTM was dead. It had been for many years. The once thriving port of entry had drawn its last breath the moment the cartels had moved in. The ice-cream parlors, shoe stores, restaurants and *tortillerías*, the hotels, discos, and bakeries had been uprooted by the drug mules, *toncho* sniffers, gun runners, *polleros*, beggars, and prostitutes. All the prosperity, it seemed, all of the goodness, had been siphoned just a couple of miles north to the suburbs of El Paso, to what the ass-kissing rags from Juárez had christened as The City of Hope. But as far as he was concerned, it was nothing more than Juárez with working traffic lights and reliable plumbing.

"What would you say if I told you that I had the ultimate score lined up?" croaked Mexicali Rose as she lit another unfiltered cigarette.

Nando's pulse began a kick-drum tempo. The fabled ultimate score, the Holy Grail for men like him: the impatient, the desperate and unscrupulous. It was a pipe dream that kept him going from score to score, promising himself like a junkie that this would be the last one, that there was another life, a slower, richer life without guilt or fear or greed. But there was always another job to do, a few more dollars to make, and it was no easy task saying no when someone had the barrel of a pistol pointed at his nuts. And yet he knew that the other life was completely plausible, but to achieve it would mean starting over, obliterating his past, regenerating himself out of nothing. He would at last have to answer a question he had posed to himself hundreds of times: What then?

A stab of lightning cracked open the sky and transformed night into day for an instant. He could see the pale and barren mountain range that stretched along Juárez's southern border, where the desert began with each pale bolt that licked the trembling skyline. The lethal beauty of the image awakened a choking, infantile fear in him, and for a moment's breath he wished nothing more than to return to the secure stone-pegged streets and swaying grass fields of his boyhood.

"One hundred five thousand dollars," Mexicali Rose pledged with a broad-blade grin that boasted a gilded incisor. "Five for the job you'll do for me, minus my twenty-five percent, of course. A hundred more for the job that's waiting for you in Chihuahua."

"What job?" Nando wondered out loud.

"What you do best," assured the woman. "There's a brand new Jaguar waiting in a ZTM warehouse with some big-shot lawyer's name on it."

"You're going to pay me a hundred thousand dollars to move a car?"

"No. I'm going to pay you five thousand. The one hundred thousand is being fronted by a woman who will meet you three nights from now in El Pajarín."

"What woman?" Nando insisted, his voice so ardent with indignation that she thought his acceptance was a foregone conclusion, and it was. He had never been offered insane money like that, not even as a joke. It had to be a smoke job.

"Relax," said the woman as she ground the spent cigarette into the concrete floor with the point of her chrome-tipped boot. "Yesterday, I got a call from Alto McKim wondering where you were and if you were willing to do a job, a big job. All he'd say was that some woman was putting up one hundred G's to have something transported to Juárez. Told him you'd be in Chihuahua doing a job for me, said I'd talk to you about it."

"What's McKim's angle?"

"I don't know what that hermaphrodite is up to anymore. Last I heard he was still trying to convert that brothel I sold him into a nightclub. Dumb fuck thinks he can turn whores into waitresses."

"Why not do it yourself? I'm sure you'll make out. Why not eliminate some overhead."

"You assume too much, *chulito.* This job smells like twenty-dollar pussy on a Sunday morning. Nobody's dumb enough to offer that kind of money for a routine transport. The fact that she did and that she insisted on you, suggests this girl is into something that a hundred grand ain't going to cover. Either that or it's set up for a bust. But hey, I told the man I'd talk to you, and I have."

There was a sudden, harsh clatter of metal, followed by the kinetic grind of a motor. The freight elevator. He followed its clamorous descent, watching the doors until they flew open in a violent rush. Two men, both clad in long, calf-length overcoats, emerged from within the darkness and edged up next to the car. One of them leaned over and tapped on the passenger window with the crown of his ring. Nando reached over and unlatched the door.

The gaunt shape poured into the car face first, smelling of hundred-dollar cologne and cigar smoke. "You Rose's man?" the voice grunted.

"Nando Flores at your service," he answered, extending his hand to the shadowed face.

"The famous car smuggler of Juárez," acknowledged the figure. "Pleasure to make your acquaintance. You'll pardon me if I don't shake your hand. You see, I have this phobia about getting infected with the microbes of . . . street people."

Yeah, and you can suck a fart out of my ass, thought Nando, yet he remained attentive and amicable as the shape occupied the passenger seat.

"I must commend your punctuality," said the shadow. "Too often these days it is a trait forgotten and abandoned. I've studied your arrival. You are discreet, inconspicuous. I think you will do very well."

There was a dry hiss, immediately followed by a murky orange plume of flame licking the thick tip of a cigar. "Your job is a relatively simple one," the voice continued, as a cloud of cigar smoke bloomed. "You will have two days to deliver the little kitten and the package to this address in Chihuahua."

He handed Nando a plain white envelope.

"What package?"

They escorted him into the freight elevator. The other man said nothing, only picked at a badly dressed wound on his forehead. They descended into the basement of the massive warehouse, where a pristine, silver-gray Jaguar XJ awaited.

"Pop the trunk," the man ordered, tossing Nando a set of keys.

"Rose said this was a normal transport," Nando fumed at the sight of the body bag in the trunk of the Jaguar. "She said nothing about . . . about . . ."

"She's not dead, only sedated. She's a little hyperactive, so we put her in here in case she woke up. But now that you'll be watching her, we can put her in the backseat. We wouldn't want her husband to think she's been treated with anything but the best of care."

"Her husband?"

"Some lawyer fuck. He ordered the car and asked us to do a little tracer on his wife, who was up here sucking some heart surgeon's *chorizo*. Said he might have us sent down the surgeon later, as soon as he raises the money."

"I'm out."

"Look, she's tied up, ankles and wrists. She'll probably sleep most of the way. It's not like you've never done this before."

"The car is risky enough. The leeches will want three times what I'll make on the transport if they make me."

"I thought you were the best. Look, it's both or nothing."

"I want the money up front."

"Payment upon delivery. That's the way the lawyer specified."

The more he thought about what was going down, the

more he felt as if he was party to a game he did not know how to play and had no business playing. It was that peanut-sized section of his brain again.

"One more thing," said the man as Nando was about to coax the Jaguar into drive. "Take this."

"What for?" he said, balancing the syringe on the pads of his fingers.

"She can be a rabid bitch. . . . Nearly bit off one of Rudy's eyebrows. Just think of it as preventive maintenance."

Just then the full fury of the storm broke and began its assault on the city.

The storm would be an advantage as most of the obsolete surveillance equipment used by the anti-contraband agents was useless in severe weather. And even if they did spot him, the likelihood that they would muster the resolve to leave the warm and dry confines of their booths or trailers for an actual pursuit was remote. As the storm raged, he began to relive the time he had taken the midnight jaunt from Chihuahua to Juárez on special orders from the mayor's son, who had managed to convince his father that it would not only be appropriate, but quite necessary to be seen on the streets of his fair city in a banana-yellow Mustang fresh off the assembly line. As the plane soared into the outer fringes of Hurricane Gregorio, diving, surging, and whipping from side to side, he had literally fallen to his knees and prayed because he was sure the plane would be ripped apart any second, and there was not a damn thing he or anybody could do to stop it. It had been his first and last plane ride.

It rained into the early morning hours. With the city far behind, the only light visible was the pale, mesmerizing glow of the car's headlamps that were beginning to play tricks on his mind, fading and intensifying, his eyeballs swimming in their sockets while the heavy hand of sleep stroked his brain. But he couldn't stop. Not until they had cleared the first check station. The storm rolled on.

Failing to make the checkpoint by dawn would be disastrous, a full day wasted because he would have to wait until nightfall to attempt the crossing again. His faithful ally, the dark, seemed to have betrayed him at that moment as he plowed the car through the wet, seemingly impenetrable night. It assaulted his senses, crowding his awareness, as he fought back the lusty promise of unconsciousness.

He reached into his pocket and took out the bottle of Tía Soyla's *chipotle* sauce. After twisting the cap off with his teeth, he sucked down a generous gulp of the peppery liquid, swigging it underneath his tongue where the burn always seemed particularly torturous. As his lips and mouth flared in agony, he caught a glimpse of his incapacitated passenger in the mirror and envied her tranquility.

What seemed like an eternity later, he saw the dove-white, almost iridescent sand dunes that signaled the approaching turnoff, the one that would allow them to evade the Villa Ahumada checkpoint. The counting game began.

There would be three high cresting dunes, after which the highway would dip into an arroyo where the actual turnoff would be signaled by one of the hundreds of roadside memorials that lined the highway. He strained his eyes as the third dune swept by. It would be coming up on his left any second. Then he saw the small wooden cross, slightly tilted to one side, buried inconspicuously on the side of the highway, the one he himself had placed there to mark the turnoff. He slowed down to verify that it was, in fact, his cross, the one whose arms bore the name of his uncle, Santos, who had given him the best advice a man could give another: Things are never as good or as bad as they seem. He slowed to exactly five miles an hour, killing the headlights of the car, and began the countdown.

In total darkness he started counting down from ten to one, timing each number with every other beat of his heart, breathing slowly and keeping his heart rate steady. Any fluctuation would throw the countdown off, and he would miss the turnoff. Trusting every fiber of his methodology, every ounce of his intuition, he spun the car into the desert. His heart froze as he felt the give of the sand, sure that he had misjudged the turn and had driven the car into one of the dunes. Turning on the headlights was out of the question. They were too close to the checkpoint. Yet if he had miscalculated the turn, the car's tires would be quickly swallowed by the sand, and they would be stranded. In daylight, the sentries at the checkpoint, as lazy and incompetent as they were, would eventually spot the car.

Then he felt the sharp dip, the one he had carved into the ground with a hoe to signal that he was on course, followed by the sweet crunch of the gravel against the tires, and he could not help but smile in the darkness, even though the night had just begun.

It would take eight kilometers of treacherous, meandering gravel road to bypass one kilometer of highway. The cars were usually smuggled in caravans of four or five at a time, carefully orchestrated by Nando, who would take the lead, being the one with the most experience. He would rely on the hundreds of times he had traversed the stretch of gravel road, on the changes in the road's texture, the consistency in the gravel, the bony fingers of the mesquite on the side of the road for guidance. The others would follow closely behind, diligently emulating the movement of the taillights, cloaked in masking tape, of the car in front of them. But this time he was alone, and things always seemed a lot more perilous when one was alone.

He could see the lights of the checkpoint floating by

as he maneuvered through the winding labyrinth of road, sweeping back and forth, sometimes overlapping the terrain he had already covered. Dawn was slowly bleeding pale light into the cobalt horizon. He guessed he had an hour to get across, no more, and he would make it, just barely, but he would make it.

Chihuahua was as dungy and wind-beaten as always, as if it had been carved right out of the barren, bronze-colored mountains that stretched across its eastern edge. He found the address that had been inscribed on the twenty-dollar bill that the man back at the warehouse had given him: a greasy, aluminum shack that tried to pass as an auto-body shop in the Niño Rey Colonia. Strange dropoff location for a his-shit-don't-stink lawyer. Last he had heard, not even the *judiciales* ventured into Niño Rey. He had been foolish enough to cross the railroad tracks into the rat-infested barrio on one occasion while searching for black-market beer after they had stopped serving alcohol in the rest of the city.

The girl had awakened once during the trip, startling him when he had spotted her sitting upright in the backseat of the Jaguar with a wild, blank stare and saliva dribbling from a corner of her mouth. Then she had blinked off so suddenly that he felt compelled to stop the car and check her vitals. Her breathing was normal and her pulse steady, but she had urinated herself. He decided to leave her in that state, even though he was forced to drive the rest of the way with all the windows down.

The spit-shined, rose-scented lawyer—real pussy magnet—was waiting in the garage alongside a man who appeared to be trying to ward off a three-day drunk in tight, grease-saturated overalls that made his crotch look like an apricot. The mechanic sauntered around the car, rubbing his chin with one finger while the lawyer peered through the tinted glass of the rear window.

"She alive?" said the lawyer, opening the door for

Nando. He was short and slim and wore the neat mustache particular to the well-educated men who fucked their wives only once a month, subsisted on a diet of cognac and *perico*, and hired nannies to wipe their kids' asses. His silver sideburns made him look older and more distinguished than he probably was.

"Alive," he repeated.

"Doesn't smell like it."

"She had a . . . an accident."

The lawyer smiled, then turned to the mechanic, and said, "What do you think the commissioner would say if he saw his beloved daughter now?" The mechanic merely smacked his lips, not the least bit concerned that he was sporting a raging erection.

The three of them unloaded the woman, who, despite the odor, the messy clothing and disheveled hair, was stunningly beautiful and appeared to be quite young. They moved her to a table inside the shack, which was dark and surprisingly neat. As he left the room, Nando caught sight of a sink containing a disposable razor, a bottle of hydrogen peroxide, a packet of large sewing needles—the kind used on sewing machines—and what looked like fishing line.

"Here's your money," said the lawyer, tossing him a large yellow business envelope.

Nando nodded, stuffing the envelope into his jacket and touching the Colt. If they were planning a takedown, it was about to be sprung.

"I'd catch a quick taxi outta here before the locals sniff you out," said the lawyer. "Then I'd find a cantina and forget what I've seen and heard these past two days."

Getting drunk sounded like a good idea, but he would not need it to forget. Another thing he had learned over the years was that a short-term memory was sometimes all that stood between a dirty blade in the kidneys and seeing the light of dawn. No, he had other pressing business to attend to before even thinking about alcohol.

The Santo Niño de Atocha Convalescent Center had been his brother's home for the past five years. This was where the city's homeless, downtrodden, and sick rotted away if they were lucky enough to have secured a bed in the ten-room, two-story building that had at one time been a technical school before being acquired by the church. His brother had been one of the center's first occupants.

Short on labor and money, the center provided marginal medical care, no rehabilitation services, no job placement or training of any kind. But who could argue with two meals a day, a bed, a weekly dab of soap with a trickle of freezing water from a hose in the basement, and a shot of penicillin once a month? Hell, he knew public servants with full-time jobs who would make that trade.

"He doesn't sleep," said Father Dagoberto as they watched Serafín tossing bits of dried tortilla to a scrawny rat. "Spends all day feeding that rat."

"Is he all right otherwise, physically?"

"It's hard to say. He doesn't allow anyone to get very close to him, much less inspect his body."

"May I try?"

"He may not remember you, and if he starts calling you Emio, you'd better step away as he may become violent."

"Who's Emio?"

"Says it's a demon waiting for him to fall asleep so that it can take his soul. That's why he doesn't want to sleep."

Nando sat on the dirt and watched his brother petting the brown rat eating the tasty piece of tortilla Serafín had laid out for him as if it was worth any risk the bleary-eyed benefactor could pose.

"How are you, *carnal*?" said Nando, still shocked at the sight of his once-vigorous older brother, whom he feared and admired, having degenerated into a slouching, dirty, unshaven lout.

"Eat it, Emio. Eat the tortilla. It is my flesh."

"It's me, *carnal*. Nando, remember?"

"Remember, that rat don't have wings."

"I want you to get better, because soon I'm going to come and get you out of here. Then we'll go to the beach, like you always wanted."

"Don't cry, Emio. It's better to bleed."

"Stop talking to that fucking rat and listen to what I'm telling you."

Serafín suddenly kicked at the rat. The rat hissed and scurried away as Serafín spat and cursed it. Turning to his brother, he whispered, "Do not sleep. Emio will come for you tonight."

"Give it time," said the priest, laying one of his large paws on Nando's shoulder.

"Fortunately, that's the one thing I *can* afford."

He turned back to his brother, who had coaxed the rat back to his side. "If you can," said Nando, "give him this." He handed the priest the syringe the man at the warehouse had given him.

"What is this?" asked the priest.

"It'll help him sleep," said Nando.

By nightfall he was blazingly drunk on a maniacal combination of brandy and beer. It wasn't that he had felt the undeniable desire temporarily to trade in his inhibitions and motor skills for a few hours of regrettable bliss. He merely felt that the monstrosity of a hangover the next morning would justify his inability to make the appointment with the mystery woman who wanted so eagerly to part with her money. Far be it from him to decline a shot at a contrabandist's version of the lotto, but not even his visit to Serafín had convinced him that it was a safe proposition. So far, the only thing he felt comfortable dwelling on was the five years he would have to serve if he was busted and convicted of illegal transport. The kind of money Mexicali Rose had mentioned usually involved something far more serious than running cars and sedated adulterous wives. It often required betting one's life, or worse, the taking of another's. There were those with the stomach and balls to fill that niche, the high-roller mercenaries and bounty hunters. He would have to wait his turn, even if it never came.

He left the Seis Botellas bar at midnight with still enough lucidity to plot the five-block walk to the downtown hospice he frequented during his visits to Chihuahua. It was nothing more than a bed under a roof next to a working water faucet that the blue-collar salesmen, low-level government employees, and freelance traders such as himself preferred during their overnight visits to the state capital. At fifty pesos a night it was a bargain compared to the wretched whore palaces, smeared with HIV and spattered with fly shit, that tried to operate as motels, or the swanky downtown high-rises that accepted only credit cards or traveler's checks.

Everything around him seemed to vibrate and shift angles. It was like stop-motion movie, and he was floating in it. In such a state of mind he could forget about the lecherous Mexicali Rose, the ball-busting lawyer who was doing God-knew-what to his wife, and Serafín's dive into that reason-deluding sludge from which few ever surfaced. Fuck it all, he whispered to the night. He had just made five thousand dollars, he was nurturing a mega-watt buzz, and was still coherent enough to negotiate—and enjoy—a world-class blowjob.

"Want to buy some beer?" said a voice from behind the thick veil of his intoxication. Nando slowly turned around, expecting to greet an old friend. In fact, a powerful sense of déjàvu came over him when he saw the stocky thug in a wool cap and sports jacket several sizes too big standing before him on the otherwise deserted sidewalk.

"Any more beer, even a sip, and you'll probably have to carry me home."

"If you want to get home, my friend, you will hand over everything you got in your jacket."

It was the sight of the knife that short-circuited the euphoria he had been feeling and replaced it with a dull, heavy nausea that made his head spin and his stomach convulse.

He reached for the Colt tucked in his waistband behind his back, but before he could get a handle on it, there was a sound like a large chunk of wood being dropped into a shallow pool of water. The last thing he saw before his anesthetized brain abandoned him was the crooked grin of the rosy-nosed punk who must have been fantasizing about all of the *toncho*—maybe even *perico* or tar—he was going to score that night.

A playful drizzle awakened him. Curled up on a park bench, it took him several seconds and a slight adjustment of his head to determine that the drizzle was, in fact, dew dribbling from the leaves of a large sycamore tree above him. At first he thought the dull pain on the back of his head was a relic of the hangover, but when he touched it and his hand came away bloody, the last few moments before he had been knocked out came flaring back.

Mexicali Rose. That was the only explanation. He was well known, perhaps even respected, even in Chihuahua, and not simply because he had grown up there. It didn't take a neurosurgeon or even someone without a hangover to realize that the most opportune time to rip off an employee is on payday.

Everything aside, there was no one to blame but himself. He should have been more careful, and normally he would have been. There had been too much on his mind: Serafín and that damned woman with her hundred-thousand-dollar job for starters. Searching quickly through the interior of his jacket to confirm what he already knew, he realized that he had failed to avoid the most dangerous state a man like himself could hope to overcome: desperation.

Injured, broke, and unarmed, he spent the morning and the better part of the afternoon walking the broken sidewalks of the park, trying to wish away the conjoined hangover and humiliation of having been taken by a snot-nose *toncho* blower. He thought about Tokyo, but he had as much chance of getting in touch with him as he did of finding the vagrant who had taken his money and killed his high. No, this one he'd have to see through by himself. At least it was a pleasant day, he thought. Without the callous, sterile mountains to tell him otherwise, the downtown district of Chihuahua was rather calming, rustically appealing, its cathedral, government palace, and museum stately, even regal. He remembered walking through that very same park as a child and looking up at the looming structures that were his whole world. Somehow, they shrank every time he came back.

Four o'clock was the earliest the city allowed establishments such as El Pajarín to unlock their doors. The smell of dank wood and diluted urine greeted him. He could detect the scent of slightly decayed yet sweetly enticing fruit, and sweat, the fast eyes and wicked smiles that had been the touchstones of the establishment's previous dealings. Some of the girls were still on hand as Mexicali Rose had claimed, trying to pass off as servants of a different kind. There was the usual assembly of alcoholics, round-the-clock hustlers, a barfly or two.

"Alto around?" he asked the bartender, who shook his head without bothering to look up from the pulp novel with a large-breasted woman stabbing her lover in the neck and the words *Amor Sangriento* on the cover.

"My name is Nando. I'm supposed to meet with him

today. Mexicali Rose sent me."

At this, the bartender dropped his novel on the counter and scowled. He opened his mouth and wiggled his tongue stump. The mute then scuttled into a room behind the liquor rack. Moments later the familiar silhouette of the blond expatriate crack-junkie, who liked to reminisce about the first time he had gotten juiced up and spent eight hours studying the carpet fibers in his living room, emerged, his shirtless body emaciated, almost translucent, a groggy grin revealing several missing teeth.

"Flower man," he hissed. "Right on time as usual. Can I offer you a drink?"

"No thanks, I drank enough last night to last me til Easter. Besides, I'm broke."

"Your money's no good here, you know that. What will it be? Dottie over there, they call her the pillow-biter. Morocco used to work for a gynecologist, has a squeaky speculum her clients call R2-D2. Patsy, the brunette by the jukebox, can do things with her tongue that would make an anteater jealous."

"I thought you were a straight-up nightclub owner now."

"Shit, if there's one truism in life, it's that you can always teach an old dog new tricks. I'm just diversifying, branching out. You ought to be the first one congratulating me."

"I'd rather just get down to business."

"Same old flower man."

"I want the job. What's the take?"

"You're talking to the wrong person." Alto stretched out a gangly limb to point toward the back of the bar, where a small shape sat hunched over one of the tables.

She appeared to have been sleeping but shook fully alert by the time he had reached her table, the feathery edges of her thick hair pouring down her neck and onto her shoulders. Her sallow face, smooth and delicate like porcelain and anchored by a pair of regal cheekbones, was small like a child's. Her mouth was tight with strong, full lips parted ever so slightly beneath a subtle yet poignant nose. Her soft aquamarine eyes, guarded by a pair of poised, thinly arcing eyebrows that seemed simultaneously charged with some ancient glory and drowned in an ocean of regret, reminded him of the morning rainstorms of early spring that swept into the *colonia* when he was a boy.

"Are you Nando Flores, the car smuggler?" she asked, a swimming hope flooding her eyes.

"Please be more careful with your language."

"Forgive me, yes, please sit down. Can I offer you something to drink?"

"Coffee."

The girl motioned for one of the waitresses, a tall redhead with bruised arms and patchy skin. "Two coffees," said the girl.

"I'm Xiomara," said this living, breathing paradox. She was elegantly beautiful yet wore the attire of a rural housewife. Appearing to be no older than twenty, she exuded a confidence and maturity that few people managed to acquire in their entire lifetime.

"I need an escort to Juárez," she finally said.

"I'm not a *pollero*."

"I don't want to get across, at least not yet."

"Then why not take the bus?"

"You don't understand. I have an appointment with a reporter who is going to help me out of a very difficult situation. There are people, powerful, dangerous people who don't want me to meet with this reporter and are willing to do anything to prevent the meeting from taking place."

"What people?"

She paused. He could see the fear in her eyes.

"What do you know about Arquimedes-Savón?"

Nando held his breath. He was more myth than man, head of one of Latin America's largest drug conglomerates, an empire of exploitation and death that practically ran the border, utilizing Juárez as headquarters for the most lucrative heroin export enterprise this side of the Great Wall, with the aid of connections, some said, all the way up the political food chain to the presidency.

"I was once . . . I belonged to his organization. I decided to leave, try to get to the North, start a new life."

"I'm a simple man who doesn't like to get caught up in things he can't grasp."

"Hence the size of the fee. One hundred thousand dollars. Cash. Payable upon the termination of my meeting with the reporter."

"I require half up front."

"I have very little money now. Just enough for the trip. Everything I have left, including your fee, is in a bank account in El Paso. The only thing I can give you now is my solemn word that you will get the full amount of your fee."

"I will need collateral."

"You have me. I'm sure you must have some idea to what lengths my pursuers will go to secure my capture. Should I fail to come through with your fee, you could ransom me for considerably more than one hundred thousand dollars. Either way, you'll get compensated."

"Do you have a car?"

"No, but I can get one."

She rose from the table and walked to the bar where the mute bartender, annoyed once again that someone would have the audacity to interrupt his visit to a world where women cut out their lovers' tracheas with butcher knives, led her into a room behind the bar, where she remained for more than an hour.

"How much did he want for this?" Nando asked as they approached the dusty, 1986 Buick Riviera that was parked in a cloistered garage behind the nightclub. By the evasive tremble in her eyes, he realized how expensive it had been and felt ashamed for having asked such a discourteous question.

Nothing of the car's interior suggested that they would have a comfortable journey. The seats were torn, the dashboard and windshield were cracked, and several small holes lined the floor. The engine turned on on the first try, however, roaring to life like a large jungle beast having been stirred from an afternoon slumber. The heavy tint on the windows would provide a sanctuary from the curious and, more importantly, the blinding heat of the sun. The fuel gauge marked a tank slightly more than half full, which would be just enough to get them to Villa Oscura, where he would have to come up with another quarter of a tank or so.

"When do you wish to leave?" he said.

"As soon as possible."

"I'll need a couple of hours' rest, but we can leave tonight," he said. "If all goes well, we should be in Juárez by dawn."

At this, she seemed to want to smile, but perhaps realized that it would have been an inappropriate gesture in such a place.

"You should take care of any unfinished business," he suggested.

"I have no business in this city," she said, and surprised him by curling up amid the tatters of the backseat and drifting off to sleep.

Ave Blanca

I was born in 1978 in a town they call Ave Blanca because of the doves that flock there every spring right before Easter. It was right around the time life started deteriorating from what had been a tranquil, if not prosperous, existence. The older, superstitious folk said that the world was coming to an end. Everywhere you looked, the signs were evident: crops were dying, livestock starving, rivers drying up. We went without rain for nine months one year. The logging companies from the North came in and began tearing away the forests. Some thought it strange because only a small number of trucks hauling wood rumbled off the mountain every week. Many believed it was just a cover for the drug cartels that wanted to use the land to cultivate poppy and coca. What little money people had managed to save over the years wasn't worth anything, with more than one hundred percent inflation crippling the entire country's economy. Everyday necessities such as shoes, milk, and medicine became luxuries that only a select few could afford.

It was also the time of the great exodus. Everyone— well, mostly the men of the village, although it was not uncommon for women or entire families to buy one-way bus tickets to Juárez or Tijuana or Nogales—started leaving, escaping to the other side and the prospect of a better life: nothing extravagant, just a respectable, honorable lifestyle, and a chance to remit a little piece of that prosperity back home. My father called them the vagabonds, and swore he would rather starve to death than desert his motherland, failing, perhaps, to realize that, at sixty-three, his days as a manual laborer were long gone.

Our family got by on what we made from the store, which wasn't much due to my father's penchant for extending credit to practically anyone who asked, but it was still more than most folks enjoyed. It was a humble business specializing in nothing, yet somehow sufficient for the needs of the simple, undemanding people of Ave Blanca. Most of the produce we sold was grown by the customers themselves, who often traded it for a slab of lard or a vial of penicillin. We sold kerosene, leather goods, candles, tabloid magazines, detergent, chicken feed, and everything else a rural village could ever have a use for. I was in charge of dispensing soft drinks. Because glass bottles were a valued commodity, rarely did we allow them to leave the store. So it was my task to pour the liquid from the bottles into plastic sandwich bags and cinch the openings shut, allowing just enough room for a straw to slide through.

I am an only child, a "miracle child," my mother used to say. The doctors told her she would never bear children because of underdeveloped ovaries. But here I am. My mother always said she could pinpoint the exact moment I was conceived. For days afterward, she could not stop thinking of snow—large, feathery crystals that coated her brain and stung her skin like a thousand icy pinpricks. She had never even seen snow, let alone touch it. That's how she knew.

My childhood was like living in a concentration camp. I was rarely allowed to leave the house, and when I did go out, it was always under the supervision of a relative or a family friend. I wasn't even allowed to play with other children until I was ten years old. They didn't want to expose me to pathogens that would devastate my already debilitated immune system. I suppose I can understand why they wanted to protect me: the fear of losing something they weren't supposed to have in the first place. It did little

to placate the resentment I began to feel for not being able
to share an ice-cream cone with a schoolmate or go to the
movies or play on the sidewalk or catch tadpoles.

When I was twelve, a man came to live in Ave Blanca.
From the way people talked about him and acted in his
presence, I knew he was no ordinary man. He built a large
church with a golden cross and a marble statue of the Virgen de Guadalupe, at the center of town. He donated
money so the district could buy desks for the students,
who, until then, took lessons standing or crouched up
against the walls of an eroding concrete warehouse. He
traveled with men with machine guns in a caravan of
trucks and shiny vans and Suburbans with darkened windows that were supposed to stop bullets. He was the closest to a celebrity the town had ever known—a living
myth, transcendental, perhaps even magical. His name
was Carlos Arquimedes-Savón.

The seclusion I had suffered as a child had diluted my
adolescence, detaching me from the social network composed of other girls my age and, of course, the boys who
started out calling them names and tossing mud balls at
them in the plaza, but who wound up buying them sodas
at the dances and corralling them into secluded alleyways
in the dark. That void was filled when I turned fifteen and
a cavalcade of men marched, ceaselessly it seemed, in and
out of my house, all of them wanting to court me. Some I
fancied, the educated, slightly effeminate boys who had
left Ave Blanca in search of a better life, returning desperate to start families and quell the growing consternation of
their parents. Others, the overly macho autocrats who
believed women require bullying and intimidation in
order to be proper wives, and the womanizers my mother
called hummingbirds because of their tendency for sticking their beaks into every flower available to them, I
quickly learned to dread. Still, my parents extended common courtesy to anyone who came calling. My mother

thought I was on the verge of becoming an old maid, as she herself had been married by the age of thirteen. My father dreamed of a good life for me, one with a caring husband, healthy children, and never a worry about what the coming day would bring.

The day Carlos Arquimedes-Savón came calling was like a religious holiday for our family. I had met him at his niece's wedding, which was attended, like all major celebrations in Ave Blanca, by everyone who was not bedridden or in mourning or otherwise incapacitated. This included the four surrounding towns of Pavoreal, Linos, Loma Cortez, and El Trueno. I had been asked to be part of the procession of bridesmaids, having known the niece of one of Carlos's business associates, Alma, since elementary school.

She was two years older than me and had become a monument of a woman whose appetite for food was surpassed only by her lust for men. She was sweet and jovial, pretty despite the girth that had been brought on by a gluttonous lifestyle. Like me, she wanted to be a schoolteacher. I had grown very fond of her since the day she illustrated for me, with a twig and a peeled orange on the church playground after Sunday school, the act of intercourse between a man and a woman. She had filled in most of the gaps in my knowledge of feminine maturity, a rite of passing that was, for some peculiar reason, left for us to fumble through by our ever-prudish parents. It had been Alma who had slipped me a tightly rolled wad of cotton after informing me of a most unappealing stain that was slowly spreading at the back of my skirt one day at school. Although not a friend in the traditional context of the word, she was, at least until the time she became preoccupied with some rather enigmatic familial negotiations, a guide through a time in my life that would have otherwise been traumatic.

That night at the reception I could feel Carlos' eyes upon me. Each time I glanced in his direction, there they were, those incandescent green eyes, so dangerous and inviting. Up until the moment he asked me to dance with him, I had enjoyed the company of various boys. When I offered my hand in acceptance of his invitation, an invisible boundary formed around us. No other men would even look in my direction for the rest of the evening, most of which I spent being swayed and spun in the vise of his embrace.

"Xiomara, you are a jewel," he whispered to me, humming along with the blaring music. I remember thinking that it wasn't the music, but his humming that I was dancing to that night. Before long he had staked out a seat at my family's table, buying beer and brandy and sodas for everybody, telling jokes and flashing that incessant, disarming smile of his, the one that always seemed to convince you that things were good, that life was worth living. He told me how I made him forget who he was and reminded him of what he wanted to be.

Toward the end of the evening, and without informing me, he asked my father for permission to court me. My father, always the gentleman, granted it.

It wasn't until the day before Carlos' arrival that I learned of his impending visit. He arrived before dinner, driving a team of horses that pulled a small wooden wagon in which he carried gifts for the entire family. To my father, who had given up drinking before my birth, he presented a case of El Presidente brandy, for which he was genuinely appreciative, as it allowed him to entertain guests for months afterward. My mother blushed like a tropical sunset upon opening the box that contained a violet saffron dress the likes of which Ave Blanca had never seen. Although she never worked up the courage to wear it, it was to be her most prized material possession until her death. For me, he brought a set of workbooks and audiotapes for learning English, admitting that he had learned that I wanted to be a teacher and perhaps even study and teach in the North.

He wasn't a particularly handsome man, except for his eyes, which were pools of a metallic mixture of green, blue, and gray that seemed endlessly deep. He made you laugh genuinely at jokes that were not necessarily funny and would talk to you as if he were an old friend who knew all your secrets, all your desires. After a while, you would find yourself telling him things you had never admitted even to yourself. He loved to tell stories of his childhood, his money, and his sins. It was these stories that solidified his stature as a living, breathing myth, an entity whose aura you wanted to taste and touch and breathe.

After dinner, we talked on the porch for hours. Carlos actually did the talking, and I mostly listened. He talked about the drought, how it was killing the spirit of the people in Ave Blanca. The government, he said, would never come to our aid because it was too busy posturing for and trying to appease the North. So it was up to us. Our destiny would have to be cultivated with our own hands. He said we had relied on rainwater for too long and that he had it under good authority that the topography on which Ave Blanca lay harbored a vast aquifer that could sustain not only the town but the entire state for decades. All that was necessary to tap it was money, of course, history's all-time favorite handicap. He knew people, wealthy people who were willing to invest in the development of the technology necessary for the acquisition of this most precious natural resource. Then he would coordinate an effort to turn the barren landscape surrounding the town into an expansive network of farms and plantations that would yield untold profits. He would build schools and clinics and soccer fields. There would be no more poverty in the region and no reason for the men to leave the village to go to the north. The government would applaud his efforts and duplicate them in other regions until the entire nation would rise up from its destitution and corruption and exploitation. We would set our own course as a people and be as powerful and independent as the once mighty Aztecs.

Listening to his ideals, believing in them wholeheartedly, wanting not only to be present when they were realized but to partake in their realization was as inspiring and mesmerizing as listening to the sermons Father Carrillo gave every Sunday morning. I decided that night, after he had left and everyone, except me, was asleep and the house was dark and silent, that I would fall in love with him. Lying there in the same bed I had slept in every night of my life, a bed—the only one my family owned—that my father had built for my mother as a wedding present, I was undergoing a metamorphosis. It was as if my life had unfolded before me and was being displayed across the gray bedroom ceiling like a movie. I saw myself and my parents living happily in a large house surrounded by orchards and broccoli, cucumber, and watermelon fields. I could see my children scurrying around and shouting in a vast playground of *zapote* trees and wild grass. I saw Carlos making love to me beneath the light-speckled sky among the lemon trees and peach groves. I can't remember when I fell asleep, but I know I was smiling when I did.

Growing up, most girls my age aspired to follow in the footsteps of the great blond rags-to-riches starlets in the photo novellas with whom we had became obsessed before we were old enough to read. So in one sense, the dream came true for me. I instantly became Carlos's untouchable girl. And although I had no more money than on the day that I was born, I was treated by the women of the village in that patronizing, mockingly obedient manner that is reserved for the privileged. The men wouldn't even acknowledge me, except to excuse themselves when they cut in front of me on the street or brushed past me at the store. There is and always will be, however, an exception to every situation. Germán Borges was to be mine.

Like Carlos, he had been away from Ave Blanca for

years. Academic scholarships and a promising career in medicine had kept him away from the traditional path most of the young men in the village followed of quitting school early, joining their fathers on the farm or in one of the journeyman shops around town, marrying a girl not more than a couple of menstrual cycles into puberty, and impregnating her every year until one of them became tired of it, physically incapable of it, or died.

Germán was handsome, not movie-star handsome or even music-band handsome, just handsome enough for a rational, moderately ambitious girl from the village to daydream about. When word got around town that he was interested in me, my image in the eyes of the village went from tenuous to downright bleak. I was no longer a prima donna, but a harlot who teased and tricked men. Unfortunately, I was too young or too foolish to care at the time.

I found Germán sitting patiently on the front porch one night when I returned from the store. He was holding a bouquet of freshly picked roses, and he smelled of fancy city cologne. I could tell that my mother liked him because she had brewed coffee. She never brewed coffee, not even for my father.

He sipped his coffee, and I smelled my roses. By the time my mother had brought out the sweet bread, he was telling me about the configuration of the human brain, about artificial hearts and frozen embryos. All the while, my father shook his head in disbelief and my mother furrowed her forehead with concern. I was sure they would have nightmares for weeks. I found myself listening as an apt pupil would to a professor, fearing that the slightest lapse in concentration would cause me to miss some invaluable morsel of information never to be repeated from his small, almost feminine lips.

He applauded my wanting to be a teacher, assuring me that the best teachers were fashioned out of the best students and that the only way to be a good student was to travel and see and experience new things. My father cleared his throat repeatedly to ensure that I wouldn't develop any crazy ideas, despite his enjoying Germán's lecture as much as I did.

Before he left, we were able to spend a few minutes alone, and it was then that he admitted that he had been in love with me since childhood, and that he always planned on returning to Ave Blanca and asking me to marry him. I was not sure how that could be, because for the life of me I could not remember him.

I was speechless, to say the least, bothered by his forwardness and incorrigibly flattered at the same time. He said he had been invited to study in a very prestigious medical school in the North and that he was in town for only a few weeks. He needed an answer fast. If I agreed, I would await his return. He had been promised a lucrative position in one of the capital's hospitals upon his return from the North. He said he wanted to get married and start a family, but that none of the city girls he had encountered was the lifelong companion he sought. He wanted someone traditional and wholesome, someone who had been raised with the virtues of the church and values wrought from hard work, honesty, and chastity.

I had only seconds to consider his proposal, but in that time I was able to plot a course for my life distinct from the fancies and fantasies that an imprudent, immature girl had up to that point toyed with in her head. While the imaginary life I had constructed alongside Carlos was thrilling and enchanting, a life with Germán would be satisfying and balanced, secure and certain. It made sense. I told him I did not love him, but that if he ever returned and I was still single, perhaps I would consider it. Crestfallen, he left, and I never saw him again.

As foolish as it would have been, sometimes I think I should have offered myself to him right then and there. I would have been obligated to leave with him that night,

his wife out of custom if not of love. In one regard, I surely would have ruined my life and tarnished my family's
name. Yet it would have been a small price to pay for the
lives of the innocent.

German never left town. His body was discovered on
the shore of the Aguacate lagoon two days later. It
appeared to have been partially eaten by some wild animal. Everyone was baffled because there were no animals
large enough to inflict that kind of damage on a human in
that region of the country. The prevailing theory was that
he had been robbed and that the perpetrators had tried to
throw off any would-be detectives from the actual cause of
death. There were other stories, of course. Some of them
even implicated Carlos, although at that time the town
was not yet ready to vilify its savior. I knew the truth. I
knew it the next time Carlos came calling.

I first noticed it in his eyes, an indictment with that
look, so full of the kind of rage spawned from humiliation.
It didn't help that he had been drinking. He talked about
death, how he was unafraid of it and how willing he was
to dispense it. It was the law of nature, he said, to die and
kill, to defend one's honor. He talked about the blood that
had been spilled to make ours a great country and that
which would be spilled in order to keep it free from tyran-
ny and the oppressive forces of an apathetic and corrupt
government. Revolution, he proclaimed, would sprout
from the agricultural fields that had lain dormant and arid
for so long. It would slip from the wombs of women who
had seen their men weep and their children die.

It was the season of the Virgen de Guadalupe, and the
entire town had gathered at the *zócalo* to begin what was
to be a week-long celebration that would culminate on the
day when the entire country would stop and honor the
holiest of our spiritual icons. The day started with the
townspeople emerging from their homes at dawn to attend
mass, after which they would enjoy the talents of the local

youth's folkloric dance groups, a parade that featured a brass band and various colorful, flower-adorned floats that paid homage to the Virgen. In the afternoon, several of the more well-to-do families in town sponsored a mole feast with enough beer to render every man, woman, and child in Ave Blanca irrefutably drunk. By the time everyone had eaten and drunk his fill, there were only a few hours left to recover before the night's grand finale, a dance featuring Los Piratas del Amor, a pop group from the capital that Carlos had contracted to play from nine in the evening until four in the morning. With a guarantee of an endless supply of beer, tequila, and brandy, it had the makings of an unprecedented gala.

Everyone was dressed in his finest garb. Sequined dresses, cowboy boots, leather vests, *norteño* hats, pearls, earrings and necklaces that blinked on and off with an electric charge. Even Gallo, the town drunk, managed to make an appearance in a clean shirt and pressed slacks, a monumental achievement for a man who claimed to have once gone three months without a bath or a change of clothes.

My parents and I sat with Carlos at a table reserved for him and his closest acquaintances, which included all of his immediate family. Actually, my parents and I were the only nonfamilial party at the table. That was something I had gathered about Carlos. With the exception of one man, he was never surrounded by anyone who was not related to him by blood.

The exception was a man named Rivas. He was a skinny, sweaty stain of a man who wore dark-colored three-piece suits that clashed with his opaque skin and ghoulish countenance, making him look awkwardly overdressed, like a man who belonged in a straitjacket, not a business suit. His salutations consisted of tongue-contorting vulgarities and the warning of an animal that would act out its impulses on a whim. He seemed to be the kind of man whose instincts had been beaten into him, branded onto his very flesh. In his wounded eyes simmered a hardened distaste for women and a lust for inflicting pain.

It was said that he had at one time been a subordinate of Carlos and that guile and ruthless ambition had ascended him to the position of minor partner in Carlos' organization. Those who looked more favorably on the Arquimedes-Savón business dealings refuted the rumors that it was a drug cartel, proposing that it was Rivas who had tainted the reputation of the town's most illustrious son. Two days before the celebration, the day after Rivas arrived in Ave Blanca, a twelve-year-old girl disappeared in the early hours of the morning on her way back from the sawmill.

Her quartered body was discovered strewn in a cactus patch outside of town that same night. All the hair had been shaved from her body, which was said to have been in a state of such despoilment that it was cremated—an act traditionally considered blasphemous—even before her parents could view it.

Most of the town blamed an alleged band of *brujos* who often kidnapped children for use in their macabre rituals. At least one other girl, however, claimed to have seen Rivas loitering by the mill that morning, smoking and flirting with some of the young women of the town.

The matrons of Ave Blanca sat quietly, smiling politely and stealing quick glances at the crowd that was entangled in a dense, oscillating knot at the center of the *zócalo*, and the men were wholeheartedly enmeshed in the ritual of inebriation. The men were like inept, newborn pups squirming for their mother's nipple, their only source of nourishment and reassurance. Liter-size bottles of Presidente brandy stood on the satin-covered tables, portents of an unruliness that seemed inevitable.

Carlos wore a crisp burgundy *guayabera* and black slacks with black shoes that sparkled even in the darkness. His hair was slicked back immaculately, and his freshly shaven face smelled of lilac oil. It felt good to be in his arms; I felt secure, potent, as if I had already conquered the days ahead of me, even though I had not yet lived them. I saw him nod in the direction of the band, and they immediately broke into a series of romantic ballads that were like a swooning dream.

I told him I was tired, and he promptly escorted me back to the table. The band had taken a well-earned break, yet the air was still electric with the voices, laughs, and utterances of the crowd that had settled in for an epic party. You could see the excitement in the frantic hands—always demanding and imploring—and the swollen faces of the men, hungry for mayhem, ready to jump at the opportunity to create it. The women, although more constrained, were equally eager for the pandemonium which could manifest itself only at such an occasion. It rose with the musky scent of their sweat, teased from their overly mischievous smiles, and poured from their eyes like the juice of a split mango.

Through the crowd came an angry voice. At first I thought it was the preamble of what would surely be numerous physical altercations that night. When it called again, more persistent this time, I could not help but turn. An older gentleman around my father's age stood at the edge of the crowd, staring directly at me. Aware that he had finally been acknowledged, he stalked toward our table. First I saw him reach into the lapel of his jacket, then his mouth expanded, lips peeled, teeth bared, the preliminary countenance of a war cry. Then I saw the gun. It flashed once as the light caught it while his wrist positioned it to lock down on the target, which, by all appearances, was me.

I didn't begin to scream until six shots had at last given the crowd what it had subconsciously been craving all night. The word quickly spread that Eugenio Borges had been shot and killed by one of Carlos' bodyguards after he had attempted to kill Carlos. The old man had apparently shot twice, missing badly both times. Rivas had responded by pumping four retaliatory shots into Euge-nio's body, killing him instantly.

The crowd formed a circle around Preciada Borges as she cradled her slain husband's head in her lap. "Why?" she screamed at the crowd, at the heavens, at anyone who would listen. "Why did you let him kill my son and my husband?"

By then the entire Arquimedes-Savón entourage had fled, leaving only my parents and me at the table. We held each other. No one dared to touch or even talk to the grieving woman, realizing that such moments were sacred and necessary. Finally, a man scooped her into his arms as two other men hoisted the corpse up and carried it off. As the woman passed in front of me, she stopped and faced me. "It is because of you that my son and husband are dead. You have brought disgrace to this town. I curse you with all that is unholy."

Carlos had vanished like an apparition. There were no more festivals, no more works of philanthropy, no parades of armored vehicles. It was as though he had never been there, except for the fact that there were three dead people and a town tormented by unfamiliar demons. The streets were deserted, the church bells silent. Even the mill was closed. Father opened the store for business every day as usual, but the only patrons we saw throughout that period of mourning were a journalist from the North and his wife who were merely passing through Ave Blanca on their way to someplace else. Slowly, after the funerals and the masses and the *novenas*, life returned to a semblance of normalcy.

The only prison more devastating than the one imposed by a court is the one that the mind creates. I had been sentenced to both. The entire town was convinced that I had caused Germán's and Eugenio's deaths. It's diffi-cult to shield oneself from such a derogatory charge, to dispute it even in one's own mind. What hurt the most was the fact that my parents had become guilty by association. Once considered among the respected elders of the town, they had become outcasts, the subjects of whispers, caricatures of gossip. My mother wept, and the buoyant light that had burned so fervently and so long had leaked from my father's eyes. Now all I saw in them was fear. For the first time in my life I became aware of the fact that he, that they, would one day die.

I spent the days locked in my bedroom, beseeching the songs and books of my childhood to release me from my penance, discovering in them only the recurring paradox of nostalgia as I sought to experience anew the fragments of a time long since spent, knowing well that I could never relive the days when the world was defined by the dew-heavy dawn and my mother's voice during a night storm. I suppose it's the kind of thing we do upon realizing that we have sloughed away childhood and that the past is forever fossilized in the well of our subconscious.

I told my parents that I was ill when they inquired about my refusal to emerge from my room. In their undaunted, resilient way, they accepted my claims without objection and tried their best to maintain the prescribed climate of the house. Fawning in episodes of self-contempt and depression, I considered running away and fantasized about succumbing to some unforeseen illness or mishap that would leave me maimed, perhaps even dead. Then they would all be sorry, and I would gloat as they tasted the tears of remorse.

In the evening I followed my mother to church, certain I would find solace there, but encountered only the indignant faces of the self-righteous crones who I'm sure fully expected to ascend to sainthood for having so devotedly graced the house of God with their embittered, high-flown presence. I could feel them spitting their prayers at my back like poisoned darts. At one point my mother arranged a private conference with Father Valverde, the town priest.

I unwillingly wept my iniquities into him, soiling his holy robes with my pain. His only response was to assure me that my distress was, besides terminal, well deserved, and that if I suffered sufficiently in this lifetime, I might perhaps find reconciliation after my death in purgatory. It was only a matter of time before my faith vanished.

Yet I was, in a sense, relieved that such a tragic era of my life had ended as abruptly as it did. Carlos, after all, was gone, as was the mayhem that always seemed to accompany him. There would be no more gilded promises and exaggerated compliments, no more conflict or reproachment, no more speculation, no fantasies about things that couldn't possibly be. Time would purge the events of that night from the collective mind of the town. All I had to do was be patient and live as best I could, knowing that the course of my life had been altered forever. All my aspirations and the possibilities that had previously seemed limitless had, during the course of a few weeks, disintegrated into a handful of pebbles to be tossed into a languid pool of water, where they would rapidly submerge into the depths of the forlorn.

No man in that village would risk his reputation by courting me. If custom held true, I would be shunned by the community and even the church, harassed by children and raped by men who thought that they were performing some act of social charity. I would be one of the Leftover Ones, a personification of the town's dark secrets, and condemned to a lifetime of loneliness and indignation.

Months passed, and slowly I began to thirst for the world again, to walk in the sun, drink in the light of day, take in the scents of the store, all the things I had taken for granted before. I started helping my mother with the laundry, feeding the chickens, and running the *nixtamal* to the corn mill every morning. I loved walking in the predawn light when the air hangs low below the dripping sky waiting for the sun's light to bleed into it. I loved the chill that turned my breath into a vapory plume and the reluctant yawn of the night as it rescinded into the tree line and riverbanks and the crevices in the earth.

That morning the load of *nixtamal* was particularly heavy because my mother had decided to prepare an afternoon feast as a sort of proclamation that we as a family had emerged from the chaos that the previous months had brought. I was to assist in making the tortillas while my mother and Berta, our closest neighbor, slaughtered and quartered half a dozen chickens to be cooked in simmering pots of *mole*. The chicken *mole* would be served with fried rice and beans on my mother's prized frosted clay plates.

As I walked through the dawn, I heard a sound off in the distance, a sound that was unusual for a town like Ave Blanca. Yet it was as identifiable as the grind of a wagon wheel or the crackle of thunder. For the life of me, I cannot comprehend why I did not, at least, turn to acknowledge the approaching automobile. As I was being plucked from the ground, all I could think as I watched the two buckets fall from my hands was that the *nixtamal* would be ruined.

They blindfolded me, wrapped my ankles together, and fastened my hands to my chest. Then one of them pinned me to the floor, planting the heel of his boot in my abdomen. When I began to cry, someone stuffed a damp rag that tasted of oil into my mouth. I can only remember that the vehicle shook and bobbed as it crossed the ragged, unstable terrain. The boot ground viciously against my pelvic bone each time the vehicle lurched. Several times I felt as if I would pass out, my nasal passages pinched nearly shut, or vomit from the acrid taste of the rag, but somehow I managed to remain lucid, reacting only when the boot dug into my abdomen.

The nightmare ended with the rasp of skidding tires and the smell of dust. All around I heard men barking, guns popping, and dogs snarling. When the door of the vehicle finally was opened, I was hoisted onto the shoulders of two men. One of them took the liberty of sliding his hands into my dress and gripping me between the thighs. It was, as it turned out, the most innocuous violation I was to suffer at the hands of those men.

The air was damp and humid and smelled of sweat, not the sweat of one or two men, but the kind that steams up in a room crammed with people. Only this room, as far as I could tell, was empty. I could hear water trickling all around, in the walls, on the floors and ceiling. Someone untied my hands and feet but quickly refastened them to supports on edges of the surface on which I lay. Then the blindfold was removed. The rest was like the apocalyptic visions that detonate in your mind during a high fever.

There were four men. They reminded me of robots. They wore sunglasses, thick shiny ones with large lenses in which I could see my own reflection. I recognized Rivas, the man who had shown up in Ave Blanca prior to the Virgen de Guadalupe celebration. He was the one who held the syringe. The others simply looked on with the manic half-grins of bad children.

"Prepare her," said Rivas.

They held me as the fat sting of the needle seeped into my arm. At first I could only hear the thumping of my own heart, escalating, rushing. It was like listening to a bass drum in an approaching parade. Then it soared, and it was no longer a beat but a massive wave crashing onto the shore of my consciousness. I was frightened that my heart would suddenly burst, but then a serenity overtook me, and I was submerged in a warm pool of water with a fragrant wind fanning my face. A froth of giggles began to stir at the top of my chest, but I held them back for fear of offending my captors. I had yet to notice that my clothes were being ripped from my body. And yet, I did not find it unpleasant to contemplate that they might do the same to my skin. I wanted to be devoured, to be ravaged and burned and bitten and wrung between the teeth of some immense greedy mouth, to bathe in its tongue, its wet hunger unfurling every portion of my being. It was as if I were two entities, one experiencing the world in real time, the other, two seconds behind, analyzing the effects of each stimulus. I could feel a thousand tiny fires igniting across the surface of my naked body. Then the voices came, dozens, perhaps hundreds of them, feminine and sweet and musical. I could feel their heat, then their hands actually touching, stroking my body. Their fingers, accompanied by water and a soapy substance, began to roam. I could feel them on my face and neck, on my breasts, hips, between my thighs, in the cleft of my buttocks. Deftly, I captured a pair of fingers hovering around my face with my mouth, and I began to suck on them, running my tongue over and between them, hoping that I could coax them into penetrating me below. But it never happened. Before I knew it, they were gone, and I was once again alone in the damp, stench-ridden room, going deaf from the blaring wind of my own breath.

I awoke feeling lonelier than I have ever felt in my life, as if I had been gutted. There was a warm throbbing in my left forearm. When I looked, the tiny blood speck where the needle had entered was still visible. I would have given my life for a few more seconds of that glorious, sensual bath. I was weeping, I soon realized, because the sensation was gone.

It was the first time in my life that I had stared at my nakedness in such a distant, clinical manner. Lying there, letting the whiteness of my body contrast with the gray of the walls, I began to shiver and sweat at the same time. It was then that Rivas walked in, his eyes hidden behind those fiendishly dark glasses.

"A virgin in every sense of the word," he said, tapping the palm of his hand with a thick, black baton like the ones used by soldiers or police officers, only his was bigger. "Carlos may be a pig, but he's a pig with impeccable taste, especially for pussy. He sees himself as a romantic, a Don Juan with the license to deflower the entire country-side. The old fool wants to procreate."

He began to stroke my leg with the baton. It was heavy and cold. I flinched, and he smiled. His teeth looked like he had been eating rotten mud. Those that weren't plated in silver, clung desperately to a receding, diseased-looking gum line. I knew I would vomit were I to smell even the trail of his breath.

"I like to deflower virgins, too," he said and flicked a button on the handle of the baton, which expanded the pear-shaped tip into four symmetrical, razor-sharp blades. "But, unlike Carlos, procreation is the last thing on my mind."

He pushed the button again, and the blades retracted. "You are in my world now, Xiomara, and there is no going back. Do all you can to please Carlos, because if you don't, he will discard you like the countless others who have come before you. Then you are mine."

By then, my entire body was shaking so violently that it seemed on the verge of tearing itself apart. And there was an aching in my bones, in my mind, a hunger and thirst combined, a need to relieve myself. Rivas smiled again, his face aglow with enlightenment.

"I have a little breakfast for you," he said, removing a capped syringe from his pocket. My body convulsed at the thought of the needle plunging into my arm and initiating that delicious mind circus.

"Show me what you feel like on the inside, then you can have your medicine."

I nodded, not even contemplating what he meant, and not caring.

There was no pain as his fingers swept into me. In fact, I could hear myself laughing as I dug deep with my body into the fire that his hand was striking between my legs. When I woke up later that day to the throbbing of my womb, faintly recalling what had happened, I felt diseased. Gone was my innocence, my womanhood having been bartered for whatever that ghoul had injected into me. I had gotten the short end of the deal, for I remembered that during the height of the euphoria I had experienced, I kept waiting for the ecstasy that had assaulted me the night before. But it never came.

Whether I had been in that room for days or weeks, I had no way of knowing. I had no concept of the passage of time. Day and night were indistinguishable. There was no light, no darkness, only the interminable gray haze over the world I perceived through distempered senses. It was during one of the dry-eyed, sour-mouthed, intermittent voids between the heroin-induced euphoria that I thought of my parents for the first time since I had been abducted. They would be on the verge of madness with worry, especially my mother with her bad heart, soaking her shawl with tears and issuing soggy laments to her savior. My father would be the epitome of despondency, a stoic automaton at the store, bagging groceries and disbursing change. At home he would rock my mother to sleep in his lap, then he would retreat to some dark, soundproof section of the house and choke out his own grief.

My lips were cracked from my constant licking of them, an involuntary response to distress that I had inherited from my mother. My eyes were nearly swollen shut from the deluge of tears. Eventually, the diurnal cycles of alternating darkness and light returned to my world, and one night, thin wafers of sweet air trickled onto the front of my brain with promises of deliverance. I was so overwhelmed with delight that I failed to notice that I was no longer in the dank prison that had been witness to my initiation, that I was lying on a sprawling, luxurious bed of satin, my body bandaged in silk and lace, and that someone was watching me from across the room.

"You are most beautiful when you cry," said Carlos.

Those green, almost serpentine eyes never blinked.

When I finally felt that I would dissolve right there in the bed or perhaps drown in my own tears, he came to my side and slid his dense arm across my shoulders.

"I have never seen someone weep so passionately," he said. "I was craving your sorrow."

"I will never be happy again," I said. "Not ever."

"We must never talk about our emotions in such absolute terms," he said. "We would be better suited predicting earthquakes than the rise and fall of our feelings."

"I've lost everything. My family, my serenity, my life. All the dreams, all the plans I had made. Gone forever."

"Tell me what you want, Xiomara. What can I give you that will make you forget the heaviness of your heart?"

"I want it to be like before, like when I was young, when my mother and father took care of me."

"That, Xiomara, is impossible. The past escapes us faster than we can remember the roles we played in it. It is like a poison slowly eating us from within, rotting our brains. It will kill us if we allow it to consume our awareness of the here and now. No, I cannot give you the past, but I can give you so much more, but you must be willing to give something back in exchange. I'd like to make a proposal that, as unromantic as it may seem now, is the result of a fondness that I have developed for you, one that I fear has been at times more evident than I perhaps would have liked it to be."

He swooped down onto the bed and scooped me completely into his arms, cradling me like an infant. His skin was creased and tinted with age. He smelled of mucus when he spoke, despite the rings of cologne that he wore around his neck and shoulders, this man who could not possibly live for more than a decade longer. He continued, almost as if he had read my thoughts.

"I am an old man with only a few years left to live. Things that were not important to me when I was young have suddenly become an obsession. The three animals have allowed me to amass more fortune than I could ever hope to spend in two lifetimes, let alone the last remaining years of my life. I have lived a full, if not righteous, life and have done everything possible for a man to do, yet there is something that I have not experienced."

Placing a hand on my stomach, he said, "I have yet to ensure that my name and my blood will live on. That is the reason I have brought you here. From the moment I first saw you, I knew that you were the one I wanted to bear my children. I have tasted many women; I have destroyed them and been destroyed by them. I have sacrificed my heart and opened my soul countless times, so many, in fact, that they have all become one big blur of stored emotions. I had lost hope and conceded to die without having left someone to carry on my legacy. That was until I met you. That day was like a rebirth. I have brought you here to ask you to be my companion, to allow me to plant my seed inside you, to take care of you and our children until I fade into the twilight."

"I want to go home, Carlos," I begged. "I want my life back."

"This is your home now," he said, his voice suddenly simmering with frustration. "If you go back, what do you have to look forward to? Ridicule, contempt, caring for your parents until they die, and dying yourself after having endured a life of loneliness? You will be the queen of my empire, with armies to command, and every desire, material or otherwise, will be satisfied. You will give me children, and I will grant you ultimate fulfillment."

By then his words had become mere formalities of inconvenience, for I was prepared to agree to anything as long as I got one thing in return. "Yes," I said. "But please give me the needle again."

"Of course," he said.

Even in the soft coma that the juice from the needle had induced, I could feel him working himself into me, clumsy and unsure. Whether it was a result of anxiety or age I could not distinguish. I just remember that I began to giggle uncontrollably as he fumbled with my legs, bending and tossing them aside like dismantled furniture. He finally managed to acquire a position that suited him, and a ripple of fear broke through the tangle of cobwebs in my mind. I recalled the night Rivas's fingers had been inside of me, and I froze at the thought of what Carlos would do once he discovered that I was not intact.

I waited, desperately trying to disguise my fear, for the moment when he would rear back in horror as he realized that his chosen breeder was not pure of body. But the moment never came. It was only after he withdrew, panting and flaccid that I, too, relaxed slightly, nauseated at the thought of having been saturated with his secretions. When I closed my eyes, I could see it glowing inside me like some radioactive seepage. Slowly, that glow began to spread from the base of my cervix to my stomach and chest, down my thighs and legs until it felt as if my entire body was aglow. Had the effects of my medicine not dwindled, I would have perhaps delighted in the sensation. But the more I fixated on the illusion, the more urgent my nausea became. I remember vomiting, then falling into a profound sleep from which I did not awaken for days.

I spent the subsequent weeks reenacting that first coupling. Sometimes Carlos would have me on the balcony outside my room with the doves on the rooftops around us. I can still hear their musical gurgle, and it was this that kept me from going insane, I believe. Once I remember lying in what must have been a large bathtub filled to capacity with warm suds that smelled like rose petals and nearly drowning as his desperate thrusts slapped the water up against my mouth and nose.

The act was always preceded by a feeding, my own whimsical nomenclature for the injections. It soon became a mundane ritual as tedious and uninspired as relieving my bladder or moving my bowels, although I rarely had the energy to accomplish even those things. Even the glow that had engulfed my body the first time he fucked me was no longer present. I was never hungry, and when I tried to take even a sip of water, I always wound up coughing it up. I was dying.

It was a month before I saw the sunlight again. One morning, I awakened to a powder-blue sky and a verdant range of foothills brooding above me. I was lying in bed on an expansive deck of milky-white marble overlooking a purple and crimson valley of glimmering avocado groves and sun-washed horizon. Heaven, I mused. It was when that familiar chill rippled across my body that I realized I was very much alive. Wrapped only in the silk sheets of my bed, I curled into a fetal position and waited for the morning sun to warm my body. It did not disappoint me as I was soon basking in its soothing wake, my naked body, having dwelt so long in the anemic trance of darkness, soaking in every last cell of the abundant light. There was only one thing missing, and I knew I could not go much longer without it.

"A bit early for sunbathing, is it not?" said the voice. I immediately recognized that subversively malignant tone and instinctively covered my body with my hands. Rivas was dressed all in white, his pants and shirt flowing loosely in the light breeze like a robe or cape, and he was holding something . . . alive. It was only after he moved out of the direct path of the sunlight that I realized it was a bird of some sort, a colorful and restless one. When it squawked, the parrot revealed its identity.

"What do you want?" I said. "Can't you see I'm in no state for company?"

"Nothing I haven't seen before, Xiomara," he said, turning to admire the breathtaking vista. "Beautiful," he pondered aloud. "If there is one thing I can say about Carlos, it's that he has an eye for the material pleasures of life.

And for women. Which is something monumental for someone who grew up with no education and in a condition more deplorable than some of the animals you will find in the menagerie he has assembled."

"What about you?" I said, surprisingly defensive, considering he was, at least superficially, not directing any indiscretion toward me. "Do you come from royalty? Are you some kind of aristocrat?"

"No. But at least I realize that no matter how much money I have, I will always be an illiterate *mestizo* from the *colonias* of Chihuahua. Nothing more, but certainly nothing less. It is this that keeps my sense of reality keen. It is this that allows me to assess the balance between my allies and my enemies and, in the end, prolongs my stay in this foolish dream we call life."

"I'm sorry, but I have no desire to continue this conversation," I said with the utmost sincerity. My body was no longer craving the tar, it was pleading for it.

"Perhaps some breakfast will lighten your spirits," he said and tossed a small amber-colored vial onto my stomach.

"What is this?"

Balancing the parrot on his forearm, he said, "Parrots are such contradictory creatures, beautiful and gallant. They are masters of illusions, efficient and unapologetic. Take, for example, their beaks, which they use to eat, breathe, communicate, and to defend themselves. And all the time we see a parrot's beak as simply a nose, forgetting that a nose, even for us, is a life-sustaining feature of our anatomy. For us the nose is no longer simply a nose but a tool of self-gratification. And yet we have the arrogance to see in this magnificent creature a mere nose. Its greatest achievement, and perhaps its most admirable trait, is its ability to convince its master that he is wise by echoing vocal tones and inflections, assuring its status as the master's most prized possession, a companion and corroborator. It could be that the animal is dumb and is only acting on instinct. But I believe that the parrot knows his owner's weakness and is bent on exploiting it until the day he sees fit to pluck out his eyes with that elegant beak."

"I need it."

"Yes, I know."

"No, you don't. I need it now or I will die."

"You will not die, Xiomara. You'll wish you would, but it's amazing how much weaker the mind is than the body. Besides, Carlos doesn't want you riding the horse anymore. He thinks it will make you infertile. He wants me to wean you off of it. He wants me to transform you into this parrot—eventually, into a little lamb."

"What am I supposed to do with this?"

"Watch the parrot. He will teach you."

The cocaine murdered the pain, despite the nuisance of taking it in through the nose and that overwhelming sensation of drowning in a giant wave of amplified light, nothing like the subtle yet potent anesthetic ecstasy of heroin. I suddenly had fathomless stores of energy and no viable outlet through which to expend it.

Carlos was almost never home, and he vanished into the shadows of the house after three or four attempts at impregnating me when he was. I began to explore the mansion, which was empty, except for the six maids and a cook. My new home was vast and extravagantly imposing, boasting every possible amenity a sheltered girl like me could ever hope to see.

The 25,000-square-foot, three-story main dwelling was a small portion of the estate that sat at the foot of a far-reaching network of hills, the result of a shifting fault line that dissected that section of the country before spilling into the ocean. I remembered being able to see it from Ave Blanca as a young girl; my father used to tell stories of the animals he used to hunt in those mountains—

deer, cougar, and bobcat.

At the south edge of the estate, I encountered a small zoo filled with every beast native to the area and a wide variety of others that could not possibly have been indigenous to that part of the continent, let alone that region. There were tigers and ostriches, spider monkeys, boa constrictors, crocodiles, and a grizzly bear. The zoo, and the entire estate for that matter, was strategically situated beneath a canopy of palm, spruce, and eucalyptus trees. A patchwork of greasewood, crucifixion thorn, bastard toadflax, and mormon tea completed the camouflage, obscuring all but the main house from every vantage point in the surrounding area, including airborne surveillance.

The entire perimeter of the estate was a configuration of closed-circuit and infrared cameras, motion sensors, and razor wire. And although I never saw an indication of any armed surveillance force, I could feel them lurking in the folds of the shadows.

There was a guesthouse at one corner of the estate that seemed too isolated to be an actual hospice for visitors. It was rather like a storage or holding pen. I never managed to get more than a few feet from its front door because it was surrounded by a twenty-foot-high, chain-link fence. The underground garage, big enough to accommodate up to ten automobiles, was completely off limits to anyone but Carlos, Rivas, and a select few of the other men. It didn't much matter, for there was plenty to see otherwise: plush, moist grass; stately shrubs; glistening ivy; bubbling fountains in the shapes of elephants, dolphins, and nude women; and multiple varieties of fruit trees. During the loneliest days I would sit on the grass watching the mangos, oranges, and nectarines ripening on the limbs of the trees, never daring to pluck any of the fruit for fear that the actual taste would never measure up to the contemplation of it.

The house itself was a three-story structure encased in a gleaming shell of white sandstone and anchored to a gradually ascending base that resembled the foundation of a pyramid flanked by looming, five-foot-thick columns. From a distance it gave off the illusion that it was floating on air. The entire back side of the mansion was a grid pattern of tall windows surrounded by constellations of smaller ones, all of them reflecting the exterior light so that they were, in essence, mirrors to the outside world.

The interior was a warren of marble, mahogany, and more sandstone. There were statues, exotic paintings, and chandeliers in every room. There were ten bedrooms, each with king-sized beds and Jacuzzis. There was a library, a theatre with a twelve-foot-high screen, a nightclub complete with a light-and-sound system, a gym, an aquarium with miniature sharks and eels and stingrays, and a kitchen stocked with more consumables than any grocery store I had ever seen.

With each step I took through the labyrinth of the house and the landscape that surrounded it, I began to experience a malevolent delight at the opulence that I beheld: a surging arrogance that made it increasingly difficult for me to consider that I, or anyone, for that matter, could live under any other circumstances. It felt as if I had been living in such a manner all of my life, that I was destined for and deserved nothing less.

Memories of my parents and of Ave Blanca soon became dream slivers that I wasn't even sure I had dreamt. I was slowly discovering that the powder Rivas gave me was nowhere near as potent or satisfying as the needle, and I was taking incrementally larger amounts of it more frequently. I couldn't eat anything except for a handful of grapes a day. The food that was prepared by the cook and delivered to my room by one of the maids went untouched. On the one occasion when she tried spoon-feeding me, at Carlos' insistence, no doubt, I slapped her hand away with enough force to make her wince and shed a small tear. I had also ceremoniously started mixing carbonated water and Presidente brandy. It became customary for me to sit on that magnificent deck, staring out into the valley of my youth, wondering if I was alive or simply the product of someone else's misguided dream.

Three months went by, and I failed to get pregnant. It had become an obsession for Carlos. Pinning my arms to the bed, he would mount me and creep into me, greedy and restless, but only momentarily. I could feel him wither after only a few frustrated grunts. Sometimes he would ejaculate; other times he would simply lie on top of me, panting, cursing under his breath. At times his exertion was so great that I pitied him, his trembling body, that pain-stricken face, and each time I began to loathe him a little bit more. His once maturely handsome face became corrugated and bristly, his mouth bloated from overindulgence, his eyes vacant and unfulfilled. Every fault, every imperfection he possessed, it seemed, was suddenly amplified.

His claustrophobic girth, loose and slick from the sweat, drowned me out like a pool of lukewarm mud. His clammy hands pulled and prodded my thighs and nipples as if looking to ignite a desire within me that would then secrete into him and augment his efforts to spill into my womb, where the fusion of life would be sparked. Instead, I was assaulted by the sensation of being suffocated in his destitution. I could feel him decaying in his own skin.

He decided that a change in venue might kindle my reproductive chemistry, so we flew to Argentina, where Carlos bought me a sapphire necklace that, he gloated, could have been used as an installment payment on the country's national debt. In Brazil we watched the last few hours of carnaval from the window of a penthouse suite that reminded me of a funeral parlor or the anteroom of a convent with its cold walls, the fragile glint of the wood floor, thick, waxy drapery, and light fixtures that protruded from the walls and ceiling like skin lesions.

There was a man in the room with us who squatted in

the shadows and chased roaches into a glass jar that he carried under a cloak of crimson velvet. One night, as Carlos and I lay prostate on the floor, our brains rippling with a harsh, unsettling opiate we had drunk earlier in the evening, he lacquered our bodies with a dark, grainy paste that smelled faintly of vanilla. Uncovering several jars full of cockroaches, he unleashed the shiny, hissing insects on our naked bodies. Carlos and I had sex as the man picked the dead cockroaches from our encrusted skin. The roaches, Carlos later revealed, were the primary ingredients in the elixir we had consumed before the fertility ritual.

I became Mrs. Carlos Arquimedes-Savón on the waterfront in San Pedro Town, Ambergris Caye, under the auspices of a local medicine man who was perhaps more stoned than both Carlos and me throughout the entire ceremony, which involved nothing more than burning incense, unintelligible supplications, and a saltwater head bath from an ivory-colored conch. In the background, an off-key clarinet and bass-drum band chased away the gulls as a group of large, tightly wrapped women traded indignant glares while their husbands passed around a bottle of cognac. I couldn't stop giggling, even when the medicine man shot a curse with his bloodshot eyes at me. Carlos was finally forced to place a hand over my mouth.

A few days later we moved into a cliff-side beach house on a stretch of California coastline populated only by a misty tree line, seagulls, and jagged, cobalt-colored rocks that looked like petrified people in agony under the continual bombardment of the angry surf. I fell in love with that sound, that whoosh of fury and sorrow, the cry of a vengeful, lonely ocean.

I was a phantasm, unable to eat, sleep, or even arrange a coherent thought. As inconvenient as the powder was, it was the only thing keeping my body going, like a machine melting down from within. My once firm and supple body had begun to sag and pale. One day I found myself frozen with shock at the emaciated specter staring back at me through the mirror. Those deeply sunken eyes and gray lips were not the features of a young woman who should have been at the peak of healthfulness; they weren't even human. I ran my fingers across my protruding rib cage and hip bones in disbelief. I was revolted and amazed that anyone could feel otherwise when looking at me, at this walking corpse that I had become.

That night I stood at the edge of the cliff listening to the waves crash against the rocks below. There was nothing beyond my feet but utter blackness and the sound of the enraged sea. I had lost everything, either by having it taken from me or by my having willingly surrendered it. So taking that final step forward seemed like nothing more than a formality, the appropriate punctuation to the brief and painful strain of my life. I had never felt such disappointment as I did when a hand clasped my arm and prevented the plunge that would have delivered me to the waiting arms of my fellow sufferer.

"Death is a bad investment," said a voice. I turned and saw Rivas's gleaming eyes. "You get nothing in return. Life, though cruel and confusing, can yield untold fortunes if one is patient and willing to sweat it out a little. Besides, death is the ultimate despot. It takes only what belongs to it. You, obviously, don't belong to it, not yet, anyway."

"You have a peculiar habit of showing up where you are not wanted," I said, furious that he had caught me at such a desperate moment.

"I just saved your life, Xiomara. I thought you'd be more appreciative."

"Don't hold your breath while waiting for me to thank you."

"You weren't such a cold reptile when I first met you. Was it so easy to forget how to be courteous or at least grateful? Physical beauty can take you only so far. It is much easier to lay waste a field of flowers, no matter how beautiful they may be, when you know that their aroma is pestilent."

"For that I would be grateful."

"I can think of a variety of more appealing things to do to you."

Pulling my arm, he impaled my face with his mouth. I struggled to get free, but his grip tightened the more I resisted. An amazing thing began to occur. A thin flame of arousal ignited at the base of my spine, making my legs quiver and my face hot. He had given up trying to engage me in a kiss and was instead exploring my face and neck, rubbing, biting, licking, smelling me. It was I who finally delivered my mouth to his. His tongue plunged deep into my throat, sucking the air from my lungs. Within seconds I had lifted my nightgown and burrowed through the layers of his suit. And there I let him explore me fully, knowing for the first time in my life the burn of lust, with the feverish ocean breeze swirling about my thighs, and the jealous rush of the waters somewhere far below.

I had missed my second period by the time we left the beach house. We arrived in Las Vegas under another cocaine-induced daze. The idea of actually being pregnant had ignited a swirling desperation within me, consuming me, hindering my thought process, debilitating my ability and will to generate even the energy to dress myself. And the only way I could temporarily abate it was to flood my nostrils with that crystalline carbohydrate that tasted at the back of my throat like overripe lemons.

It was sensory overload the moment we stepped out of the helicopter. And it wasn't just the lights or the surreal collection of ornate monoliths that bled pulsing rivulets of sooty purple, ultraviolet green, and tracer beads of amber that animated the skyline into a parade of concrete, glass, and neon. It was the people, their laughter all around me as if they were in agony or perhaps drunk from the sweaty stench of money. It was the vertigo as cars flew down the streets, wailing in protest, at suicidal speeds. It was the artifice, the façade, the air that tasted like it had been cured with an electric current, broiling skin and bone beneath Ray Bans, Versace, and Hawaiian Tropic. The lip gloss and mascara ran, the cologne and hair spray evaporated. It hurt to be awake, yet falling asleep was impossible with my heart laboring double-overtime and my brain filled with apocalyptic images of the end of the world. So I closed my eyes and sipped my brandy and listened to my body weep.

"I think I'm pregnant," I said to Carlos as we dressed for a dinner date one night when it felt as if my mind was boiling inside my skull. Having not touched me in almost three months, he froze in mid-tie knot. I could see the disconsolate look in his eyes as he stared into the mirror.

"I thought you'd be happy," I said after failing to solicit a response.

"I didn't want it like this," he finally said. "But I suppose the only person I can blame is myself."

"What are you talking about?" I half-screamed, incredulous at his apathy after the countless nights of lying beneath him, playing the role of receptacle for his desperate, geriatric dreams, submitting to his accusatory stares that negated even the possibility that my inability to conceive was not my fault alone.

"I didn't want a breeder," he said, securing his tie. "I wanted a mother for my children, Xiomara, someone to care for them and love them and nurture them. It's bad enough that you have created a chemical baby. How can you be a mother when you can't even change your own diapers?"

"Is a drug-trafficking father any better?"

"Don't say things you know nothing about. But I suppose your brain is cluttered with all sorts of delusions and paranoia. Perhaps even this pregnancy is another hallucination brought on by your nose food."

"You took me from my home, my family, from friends I will never see again. When people used to talk about Arquimedes-Savón like a disease, I defended you. When they said you sold drugs and enslaved your people, I told them you were only trying to elevate them from misery, that the end justified the means. When they said you were a murderer, I told them you were a saint. I was a fool."

He winced, tugging lightly at his lapel, but I was relentless.

"I'm not some freshly picked, dull-witted flower from the countryside. Not anymore. So you can spare me the condescending discourse on what I do or don't know about what my beloved husband does for a living."

I was breaking apart. Unable to sustain the weight of my torment, I collapsed onto the floor, crying shrilly for my mother as I had done when I was a child. At that moment I yearned for nothing more than to feel her warm breast against my face or smell my father's firm, tobacco-scented hand as he stroked my hair. Yet I had come to the realization that they were gone forever, and that even if I were to see them again, we would all be strangers. It was this that hurt more than anything.

"I'm sorry," Carlos said, lifting me onto the bed, a quivery sob tugging at his voice. There was a split second of volcanic joy as my gullible mind mistook his voice for my father's. "I have neglected you. How trying this must still be for you."

Choking back my sobs, I lifted the vial I always carried with me to my nostril, but he quickly swiped it from my hand. "No," he scolded. "If you are truly pregnant, Xiomara, we must do this right. We will see a doctor first thing tomorrow. In the meantime, we've got to get you off of this and get some food into you. And stay away from Rivas. He is a serpent. Every day I find myself trusting him less. I fear he might . . . try influencing you in negative ways."

His words felt good, and I believed him. We blew off

the dinner date and ordered room service instead. He spoon-fed me soup on the balcony of our room while we watched an intricate array of water cannons shoot jets of mist and foam into the air.

I was for a time emotionally sated, content to believe that a normal life could be possible. The prospect of having a child, a true marriage, and a family elated me. I tried to purge myself of the need for the powder. I was clean for about two weeks. When at last I began to feel my body change, to experience that metamorphosis that feels at once so natural yet so terrifying, when I began to feel it growing inside me, it became unbearable.

I was in a continual maelstrom of nausea, tremors, and hysteria by the time we arrived at Carlos's desert stronghold, an isolated, half-interred bunker that ran on solar and wind energy. The only way in or out was by helicopter, as the treacherous landscape, one of the location's many strategic defense features, allowed only vertical takeoffs and landings. Everything, including food and water, had to be flown in. Anyone foolish enough to attempt a ground incursion would perish from the heat or a bite from one of the deadly reptiles that infested the rocky cliffs and lava beds long before sighting the dome-shaped crown of what Carlos lovingly called Hell's Whisper. Rivas had picked up the scent of my desperation. I could see it in the droopy smile he strung up as he watched me from across the room. I was his, and he knew it.

"I hear you are of the black bow," he said one morning after Carlos had unexpectedly flown out. "Congratulations."

"I don't know what you mean."

Not bothering to lift his eyes from the screen of his laptop, he said, "In the time of the Aztecs, women would wear a black bow to communicate the fact that they were pregnant. They would be regarded as sacred—walking miracles, in fact."

"I don't know whether to be ecstatic or delirious."

"Well, if it's advice you seek, you've come to the wrong person."

"I'll trade all the advice in the world for a couple of drops of medicine."

"Carlos would rip you open if he knew what you were asking of me."

"You mean both of us."

"I am no one's victim, not even of the great Carlos Arquimedes-Savón. Maybe once, but never again."

"I don't care. I'm dying."

"You would risk the life of the child you carry for a few moments of artificial pleasure? I knew there was a reason I liked you, Xiomara."

"Fuck off. Give it to me or I'll tell Carlos that you raped me."

"Provincial bitch," he spat, lunging at my throat. "Did it ever occur to you that the wad of cum mutating inside you is probably mine? In fact, I have no doubt that it is. You know it's true. You just refuse to believe it because you are so obsessed with this idea of giving that impotent old fool his last wish. The next time you threaten me, I will cut out that tumor from your womb and feed it to you piece by piece."

He shoved me against the wall and tossed a syringe at my feet. "There," he said. "I've changed my mind. I'm going to enjoy watching you rot."

The sweet numbing of the brain was there, as was the sensation of a vast expanding universe full of color and light, so much light, but gone was the maddening delight of those first times when I thought I would die from the sheer pleasure and was content to do so. But that didn't stop me from trying to recreate it. It was all I could do to fight off the aftertaste of Rivas' words, the knowledge that I was carrying the child of such a creature. He was right. I had known all along but had repressed the thought. I had not been with Carlos for almost a month prior to my encounter with Rivas. Yet that stupid, naïve part of me had entertained the notion that I was finally going to make Carlos' greatest desire come true, the one that neither his money nor his influence could purchase.

A regiment of Ciudad Juárez municipal police was waiting for us as we landed on a private airfield outside the city a week later. The pilot took a bullet in the head as he jumped from the cockpit to stem the stampede of gun-toting soldiers. Mowing down the pilot's body, they surrounded the helicopter and waited for one of us to make a fatal move.

We were herded into the back of a military-style Humvee and hauled to a remote training facility, where Carlos and I were separated, placed in separate cells, and interrogated by a trio of sleepy, disheveled men looking for anything to kill their boredom. They smirked when I disclosed that I was pregnant and submitted me to an examination with a flashlight and a video camera. I was assured that the footage would be reviewed by a doctor who could confirm whether I was with child or not. It was hours before they allowed me a drink of water. After nearly passing out from exhaustion, I was finally allowed to dress and lie down on the damp concrete floor.

I could taste the rage that was building up inside me—the raw, gamey hatred that one human being can develop for another. I hated those men for their utter disregard for my dignity. As I listened to their moronic laughter and witnessed the sadistic delight they extracted from my degradation, the only emotion my roiling mind could consent to was the desire to exact a vengeance against these brutes who had violated me. I not only wanted to punish them, I wanted to annihilate them.

Carlos had been forced to watch my interrogation via short-circuit television. A fictional conclusion in which I was raped and beaten to death was edited into the playback, so for hours Carlos thought that I and the child inside me were dead. I could only wonder about the identity of the woman who had actually suffered the fate I was spared. Rivas had left the desert compound a day before our departure, and it was days after he arrived with orders from the municipal judge for our release that Carlos managed to convince himself that the child and I were alive.

He was never the same again. Even on the morning when we went up in the helicopter to watch an unmarked F16 direct a pair of laser-guided missiles into each of the buses that carried the men who had arrested us at the airport, I could tell that part of him had died, that a portion of his sanity had been compromised. He sat stoically as the missiles hit their targets, shooting stadium-size fireballs into the air, while I screamed with vindication and regret that I could not make them relive the moment when their bodies were singed to oblivion over and over again.

According to Rivas' debriefing, someone, probably operatives from the Baja-Cruz organization, Carlos' most formidable adversaries, had tipped off the Juárez municipal police about our itinerary. Word was that they were positioning themselves for a run at the *permiso*, which would be awarded as soon as the new president was sworn in; they needed to get Carlos out of the way for good. The *permiso* was a tradition of the ruling party that dated back to the days of the first opium runs put out of the coastal valleys of western Mexico. It was the unspoken endorsement issued to a cartel that was particularly loyal to Los Pinos. It guaranteed the cartel safe passage of their cargo and their operatives immunity from prosecution provided, of course, that adequate compensation was offered to the stewards of such a lucrative entitlement.

Carlos felt that it was time for me to leave. He foresaw that the violence would escalate between the Arquimedes-Savón and Baja-Cruz organizations, and he feared that they would try to get to him through me. His act of vengeance had been symbolic not only of his willingness to engage Baja-Cruz in a blood war, but also of his disparagement for the Baja-Cruz brothers as men of integrity. Even in such a brutal world, honor was still regarded as the variable that separated men from beasts. To challenge someone's honor was to deny that person's status among his peers.

I was almost two months along when I arrived at the coastal village of Playa Verde, escorted by Rivas and a new man who was never more than three steps away from me, even when he was nowhere to be seen. I was a guest at a seaside hacienda called The Orchid, which was apparently run solely by an elderly woman named Marina, who cooked, cleaned, washed, and, by all accounts, protected the majestic, ten-room villa that I was to call home until informed otherwise. She also rubbed my feet with alcohol and prepared strange yet invigorating potions that I drank every morning and night. I found that they diluted the high I was scoring thrice daily, but rendered in me a peace of mind I had not felt for God knew how long.

She rarely spoke, and our infrequent conversations consisted of her inquiries about the condition of the little cub, as she called it. I would respond by assuring her that he—or she—was fine. She would smile approvingly and disappear into another room to continue the seemingly endless housekeeping chores. Her face, under certain types of light and from distinct angles, was familiar, although I could not guess how I could have possibly encountered her before. Then it occurred to me that she was related to Carlos.

"His sister," confirmed Rivas, who would never set foot on the property. "She's going insane. He bought her the hacienda to keep her mind occupied. What's left of it, anyway. And it's a good place to disappear. Not many people have ever heard of Playa Verde. Carlos has always worked to keep it that way."

"Did he tell her I was pregnant?"

"Yes. If you ask her, she'll probably tell you she divined it. She despises me as much as I do her. She will start in on you with her spells and superstitious bullshit as soon as she knows I am far away."

"I thought you believed in such things."

"I did once, but I've learned that it's dangerous to believe in things you can't control."

"When do you leave?"

"Tomorrow. Don't worry, I've left Prado fully stocked and have given him all the details of your . . . prescription."

"Pity you can't stay. I mean, if you ask Carlos, I'm sure . . ."

"He'd know I was fucking you for sure."

"I forget."

"What?"

"That you are incapable of virtue, that you are a cold heartless man who cares for no one unless it serves his interests. It sickens me to think that the child I am carrying might even remotely resemble you."

"Whatever species of creature you have designated me to be, you must not forget that you are one of us, Xiomara, just like Carlos and me and all of them."

"He is *not* like you. The light that was extinguished from your soul burns within him. He can still love and long and dream, even if they are the sad, desperate whims of a fading man."

"Let me tell you about your beloved Carlos Arquimedes-Savón. He has humiliated and violated women with impunity, executed men in front of their weeping sons. He has laughed in the face of God by breaking every one of His commandments. He has pissed on the land of his countrymen and poisoned the blood of those closest to him, even his own child. All to ensure that his fortune will flourish, that his empire perpetuates. At this very moment, with the aid of those he employed to massacre the two busloads of Juárez police, he is planning the extermination of the man who aspires to take the reins of this faltering country, a man whose only flaw is that he has already vowed to do everything in his power to unseat Carlos from the top of the clandestine hierarchy. To your husband, his will to power is more important than the fate of millions of his countrymen. That light you talk about does not seem to shine as brightly within him now, does it?"

There were days when I experienced immense joy at the thought of giving birth. Then there were moments when I remembered the conversation I had had with Rivas before he left. It was during these times that a great anxiety overcame me. It began with a nervous tremble at the pit of my stomach. I could feel my blood pressure rise and my heart begin to quicken. Before long, my limbs had gone numb, and it seemed as if I were looking at the world through a small, yet thick window. I thought I was going to die. I would lie down, sucking in air, trying to calm my racing heart. It would eventually pass, but I knew that the respite was temporary and I dreaded the moment when the darkness of my wrecked mind would take flight once again.

My only escape was the languid kiss of the ocean on my feet as I walked the beach. Riding on the high of the heroin, I floated across the swift, tepid breeze that spun off the waves at dusk, my restless toes molding the creamy sand. It felt like the entire force of the rising ocean was swelling up inside me—the palm trees swaying and thrashing in my head—that I would suddenly come undone as the magnetism of the water burst out through me. The sensation was shorter each time. When it was over, I would have preferred death to the empty sounds and translucent shadows that awaited me at the hacienda.

Prado was always off in the trees or bushes, keeping vigil over the property. The old woman still continued to nourish me with her soups and potions. The teas were pungent, yet sweet enough to be tolerable, despite their wretched green consistency. I enjoyed the soups more. There was always a lemony tang to them that resembled *anis* or chamomile. Some contained flower petals or bits of some strange root. Others were white and creamy with grains of a long, broad type of rice that was unfamiliar to me.

I lay in bed one day staring at the patterns of texture on the ceiling that resembled human bodies entangled in violent or intimate embraces. I didn't even hear her come in until she was standing right above me like some large, dark bird. She leaned into my face with those swollen, droopy lips, smoky eyes, and the smell of sorrow.

"I will bring it out," she whispered.

I barely had time to gather another breath when she stuffed something wet and slimy into my mouth. It was cold and tasted like a rotted vegetable. When I tried to spit it out, she clamped my mouth shut with both hands. I could feel things oozing out between my lips and the corners of my mouth as I tried to fight her off. Her strength was stifling. I suddenly realized that if I did not swallow the thing, I would choke. It squirmed down my throat as if it were alive. When I at last stopped fighting the woman, she relinquished her grip and left the room.

Had I possessed the strength, I would have wept, but I suddenly realized that I no longer had control of my body. It had been drained of all its energy, and a heavy cloak had fallen upon my mind, rendering everything I was feeling and seeing in slow motion. The only thing that still seemed to be functioning normally was my heartbeat, which reverberated throughout my body as if it were being wrung through a loudspeaker.

I was faintly aware that something was happening between my legs, but I didn't even have time to become alarmed because the next thing I knew I was lying in a shallow pool of warm water. There was pain, and it intensified when I tried to move, so I remained still as a pair of tender hands dabbed water on my shoulders. When I finally managed to open my eyes, I saw that the water was red.

"Blood," I croaked.

"It is gone," said the old woman. Her voice was the only thing that confirmed her presence, as the rest of her remained unseen. "You are one again."

"I don't understand."

"The unborn child. I took it from your body and threw it into the ocean."

"God, no!"

My mind was a white-hot kettle of rage. I did not want to kill Marina. I wanted to disembowel her with my teeth, to shred her breasts with my fingernails and pour scalding water into her eardrums, to arrange some time for her in a small room with Rivas. In that instant I was peering into the cavernous undercurrent of his heart, and I drank from it the cold, shimmering desire to inflict pain. I was nauseous with it and aroused at the same time. But I could do nothing as the pink, warm water washed over me.

"You were infected," she said. "Now you can seek redemption."

"Foul, wretched creature! You are the infected one. You have destroyed the only meaningful thing that was left of my life."

"You may think that what I have done is an abomination. The child was already poisoned, and he was poisoning you. He would have brought that poison into the world, just like the man who engendered him."

"How could you say such things about your own brother?"

"That child was not of Carlos' seed, but of that man, that beast who brought you here, the one who calls himself Rivas."

"How did you know?"

"The same way I knew that by taking one premature life, I would be saving the lives of countless others."

"But it was going to be Carlos' child, the one he always

wanted. How could you have destroyed the dream of your own brother, the one who feeds you and protects you?"

"He is the one who imprisoned me. My brother can never have children. Never could. He was born impotent. I told him long, long ago. It was one of the many reasons he put me here. He thought I was crazy, that I would shame the family, the family I was never quite good enough to be a part of. And yet I was still too good for others, the men who wanted to marry me and give me the life I was never meant to have."

"And so, in your bitterness, you deprive others of happiness."

"No wonder you fell so easily into the web. There would have been no happiness. The misery that you have endured, Xiomara, is nothing compared to what awaited you. That child would have grown to commit unspeakable atrocities, and you would have borne the burden of your son's sins. You would have carried the guilt and ultimately suffered the punishment for them because that would have been your duty as a mother."

By then, her words had become pockets of empty space in the air, the water against my skin the thin membrane that separated reality from the subconscious, and I slipped into whatever lay beyond the mirror-smooth plane of my anguish.

What followed were slow, uneventful days in the dutiful hands of Marina. Her tonics kept me sedated and allowed me to keep the demons of my despair at bay. At times I would cry and not realize it until the old woman would come to my side and place my head in her lap and stroke my hair. Sometimes she would lift my chin until my face was almost touching hers and brush the tears from my eyes with her cheeks. When I opened my eyes, I would see my mother, and she would smile and I would cry out from sheer joy.

I bled for several days, the blood gradually becoming

darker and thicker until it became a smattering of black clots. They stopped around the same time that I came out of my stupor. By then, Marina was constantly talking whenever I was in her company. Even Prado was surprised when he frantically appeared at my bedroom door, ready to take down the unfortunate individual who had wandered onto the property and into my room to strike up a conversation.

She told me of the loneliness that accompanied her throughout her childhood, a loneliness that had started as a result of an experience that had either given her the gift of what she called transcendence or simply revealed to her a power she had brought with her from the womb. It happened when she was six years old. She had been sitting under a guava tree. Most of the guavas had already been picked. The ones that hadn't were scattered on the ground rotting and being devoured by insects. Yet a single guava remained high up on the tree, its golden skin flesh shimmering in the sun. Eager to get at the plump, juicy fruit, the last and best of the season, she climbed the tree, scratching her face and small legs against the sharp, hard branches. When she had at last reached it, she did not bother to climb down but began to devour it right there on the limb of the tree, taking it entirely into her mouth to crush it with her tongue and the muscles in her cheeks. As she was bringing it to the roof of her mouth, it slid past her tongue and became lodged in her throat.

A wave of panic rose from behind her eyes, drowning out everything except a peephole through which she could still see her hands trying desperately to cling to the tree branch. It was no use. Her strength and balance waned as her oxygen-starved limbs finally gave. It was then that time seemed to pause. Everything, including the breeze that had been rattling through the leaves since earlier that morning, was suddenly still, and there was silence all around. Even the sunlight seemed affected as individual shards of green, blue, and orange light burst just before they struck her face. The most incredible manifestation, however, was the fact that she had stopped falling and remained hovering inches from the tree branch she had been clinging to only seconds earlier. She was no longer choking. She could still feel the guava stuck in her throat, but a warm glow had overtaken her body. Suspended in midair, she watched as a giant golden eagle soared out from behind the tree and dove toward her. It clutched her by the shoulders and pecked the guava from her throat with its beak. The next thing she realized was that she was lying on her back gasping for breath at the foot of the guava tree.

She told me about Alberto Savón, Carlos's father. Being the only boy in the family, Carlos had suffered the full wrath of a demanding, strict, and overbearing father, who ignored his wife, except for three times a month, and treated his three daughters, like servants prescribing either a destiny of perpetual submission to his iron will or the convent. But at least they were never beaten—an honor reserved for the only son. However, he did threaten them with a swift death should any of them display the slightest sexual inclination.

Carlos, on the other hand, looked forward to the daily struggle of proving his manhood to his father. If he failed to do so, he would be kicked and flogged and thrown around like a dust rag while being called *maricón*, woman or cunt.

Alberto Savón died at the hands of his oppressed son. Despising Alberto, a man they had always regarded as uncultured and tyrannical, the Arquimedes family rewarded Carlos with a position in the family's export business. Carlos, his mother and three sisters moved onto the family estate, and it wasn't long before his father's ruthless, sometimes cruel, nature began to manifest itself in the boy. But as Alberto's personality proved to be detrimental,

and eventually caused his undoing, for Alberto, for Carlos
it was an asset. He was soon managing the regional distri-
bution for the family business, which included the chan-
neling of goods such as farming tools, automobile parts,
and produce to the neighboring states. It wasn't long after
that he broke into the more guarded, prosperous, and
nefarious side of the family trade, a part of the business
normally reserved for the closest kin. This involved running arms into the southern states, stockpiling unregis-
tered antibiotics and various unidentified chemicals that
were bound for processing plants in South America.

It had been Carlos who proposed to the family the
idea of venturing into the emerging opiate trade. Within
two years, the family had nearly quadrupled its fortune. It
was also about the time that Marina, the oldest daughter,
became interested in the opposite sex. She was thirty
when she began sneaking out at night to see a man from
one of the neighboring farms.

By then, Carlos had garnered so much prestige and
influence within the family that he was rarely, if ever, chal-
lenged on any decision or action, not even by his mother.
One night, Marina had had enough, and she confronted
her brother, disclosing to him in front of nearly the entire
family that she had not only been seeing a man, but had
surrendered her virginity to him. Carlos promptly summoned a doctor and ordered him to verify his sister's
assertion. When the doctor determined that Marina was
no longer a virgin, Carlos ordered him to perform another procedure upon her. It involved the mutilation and dis-
figurement of Marina's sex to such an extent that she
would be ashamed to show herself to anyone, let alone a
man, again. She nearly died from the ordeal, and Carlos
got his wish. The other two sisters were so shaken that
they fled to a convent, just as their father had ordained.
But Marina stayed on to care for their mother until the
matron passed away.

It was then that she found herself alone in the world. Almost fifty, she pleaded with Carlos for a place of her own, a place where she would be isolated from the rest of the world yet in harmony with herself, a place where she could grow the herbs and flowers she loved, a place where no man would ever set eyes on her again. With most of their mother's relatives having died or grown too old, Carlos had risen to the head of the family business. He had amassed a fortune worth billions of dollars and the power to do as he pleased. In exchange for surrendering one of his lieutenants to the drug police from the North, the government granted him an oceanfront property that had been used as a retreat by prominent political officials. This was his gift to his beloved sister, proof of his love for her despite all the burdens he had imposed upon her.

One day she said something that made me think that she had, indeed, gone slightly mad. "My brother will perish, and you will take his place," she whispered into my ears as she kneaded dried corn kernels from a stack of cobs at her feet. When I tried to coax an explanation out of her, she hid behind a faded shawl and an off-key hymn.

Another night my mother came to me, or rather, I went to her. I was sitting at her bedside, and she was weeping for me, only there were no eyes on her face; they were on her forearms, the insides of her biceps, her thighs, and tears were streaming from them. They were tears of blood. I awoke feeling as if a scythe had been drawn across my breast, waiting solemnly for the dawn to arrive.

With it came a mournful Marina. The sun had yet to break, but even so there was a shimmering in her eyes like the tears in the ghoulish face of my dream mother. "Xiomara, you must go," she told me. "Your mother is calling you."

"What do you mean?" I implored. "Is she ill or in danger?"

"I do not know. I can only hear her desperate voice

calling your name. She is sad and alone."

"She is ashamed of me. They all are. And why shouldn't they be?"

"She came to you last night, didn't she?"

"Yes."

"Then you know my premonition to be true. She came to me as well."

"What did she say?"

"Nothing. She was asleep in the arms of the man."

"What man?"

"Her Savior."

I wanted to run from the shell of my own being, for I knew that two such portentous visions about the same person could not be a good omen. In fact, it could only mean one thing: my mother, or someone close to her, was dying.

"I cannot take you," affirmed Prado. "My orders are to keep you here until I receive word from Señor Rivas."

That night as he was succumbing to the sedative Marina had mixed into his food, I stole into the jungle and made for Playa Verde, using a crude map Marina had etched for me. In town I paid an off-duty policeman to drive me to the nearest bus station, almost three hundred miles away. I had left everything behind except what was left of my hundred-thousand peso monthly allowance and, of course, a week's supply of injections that I had stolen from Prado's car just before I left. I slept for most of the two-day bus ride into Ave Blanca, oblivious of everything, including the purpose for my impromptu journey.

I arrived just after sunset and found a small crowd gathered outside my parents' house, some of them drinking coffee or smoking, or just standing amid the shadows of the waning day. They stared at me distastefully as I stepped out of the taxi. Having not bathed, eaten, or changed clothes in almost two days, I concluded their scornful facial expressions to be the result of my appearance rather than disdain for my presence. Most of them probably didn't even recognize me. I bolted past them through the narrow door that had framed my childhood and early adolescence. The room was dark, hot, and smelled of melted wax and stale prayers.

My father was sitting at the side of his and my mother's plank-and-straw bed surrounded by relatives I had not seen since I was a small girl. No one had acknowledged my arrival. Their drawn gazes were fixed on my mother.

She appeared to be sleeping peacefully, her eyes tightly shut, her mouth slightly ajar. My head swelled with relief when I saw her chest rising against a shallow rhythmic breathing, but there was nothing else that indicated that my mother was or would be all right. Suddenly she opened her eyes, turned her head, and stared right at me. It all came flooding back, every embrace, every argument, every meal she had prepared for me, and the dresses she had sewn, the hair braids she had crafted, and her gallant walk across the courtyard. She smiled then, and it was like a pink, soothing light that went straight through me. I collapsed onto the bed next to her. I wept out of sheer joy of being in the presence of the glorious woman who had brought me into the world and who, despite my debased life, still loved me enough to expend her last ounce of strength to smile at me. When I looked up at her again, the smile had faded, and my mother was dead.

All I can remember of the days that followed were the countless faces, bodies, and hands, reaching for me and my father, offering condolences and prayers. I was riding a continuous wave of heroine-induced indifference. They all looked the same to me, men and women, old and young, their words echoing the ones that came before and those that would come after. I neither ate nor slept, but simply waited for the crescendo to ebb so that I could jack it back up with a fresh injection. It wasn't long before I was down to my last couple of fixes.

Somehow, through the haze of my mental anesthesia,

I managed to bury my mother. At night I would hear my father's soft howl somewhere in a corner of the house. He would talk to my mother, call to her, beg her to come back to him, and promise to wait for her until she did. Two days later, the cemetery curator found his lifeless body curled upon my mother's grave. It was then that I injected what remained of the heroin I had taken from Prado, wanting nothing but the void that awaited me as my awareness evaporated into the sky.

The light was impaling my eyeballs, but I was awake and feeling invigorated and sound of mind. Carlos was at my side. I heard the shy rustle of his weight on the bed. After dry kisses, painful embraces, and a stream of tears that seemed overly dramatic for him, he recounted how he had sent for me after hearing of my mother's passing. He panicked, thinking that Baja-Cruz had located The Orchid when they discovered that I was missing. Rivas had executed Prado for his incompetence and hired a team of locals to comb the area for any trace of my whereabouts. He soon received word from one of his spies that I was in Ave Blanca. His men arrived at my parents' house shortly after I had overdosed. For two weeks I had remained sequestered in a locked room, where I was fed intravenously by a local doctor who was amazed at the intensity of my withdrawal episodes. At one point the doctor, being the voice of experience and prudence that he was, suggested to Carlos that I be put out of my misery and tossed on a roadside or into the bottom of a well. After all, there was nobody left alive who would care.

The doctor assumed that I had suffered a miscarriage as a result of my heroin use. Carlos took comfort in the fact that there was still time for us to have a child, and urged me to stay clean, but he made no inquiries as to where I had obtained the heroin. I supposed it was easy enough for a woman in my position to obtain. I figured that in his eyes, Rivas was still above suspicion, at least in that regard.

The weeks passed, and I slowly began to adjust to my new life, to the realization that I was an orphan, that I was no longer pregnant, and that I was clean at last. Everyone around me seemed to have undergone his own transformation. Rivas was rarely seen at the house. The guards and the maids were more reserved and colder when they interacted with each other and with me. Even Carlos seemed more on edge than usual, almost to the point of paranoia.

I attributed this imbalance to the tumultuous political climate and the impeding presidential elections. A brash, idealistic candidate from the southern provinces had vowed to instigate sweeping reforms that would expunge corruption from the political and social fabric of the nation. Recent polls indicated that the candidate, Benigno Juárez, was making headway and was, in fact, poised to challenge the ruling party for the presidential office.

"These are dangerous times," Carlos said to me as we walked the grounds of the estate one evening. "I fear that the stakes are becoming too high and that I can no longer accept the responsibilities and the pressures of my reality."

"You've always triumphed," I said, feeling rather uneasy that the man, who since I had known him would have surrendered his life rather than his pride and reputation, was talking like a wounded soldier on the verge of surrender. "And you always will."

"I used to believe that," he said, finding solace in his cigarette, "when I was young. Things are so much different now. The people, politics, the game. I must confess something to you, but you must swear on your life that you will never repeat it. The fact is, my life and yours depend on it."

I nodded, dreading whatever it was that I was about to hear, but knowing I was powerless to prevent it from passing through my ears.

"Benigno Juárez will not live long enough to cast his own vote. As we speak, there is a squadron of assassins being trained to carry out his murder. I was asked to make the arrangements, but I refused. Even at my age, there is still hope in my heart for this nation to be great one day, second to no other, including the colossus of the north, to bring all of those things I've always talked about to fruition. Even though I cannot stop this calamity, I refuse to take part in sabotaging my country's future."

"Then who is training the assassins?"

"Rivas. Who else?"

"But how can that be? He works for you."

"It's not that simple, not anymore. You see, the ruling party is not willing to relinquish power to an upstart such as Juárez, even if he is elected by the people. They have promised that whoever carries out the assassination will be awarded the *permiso* to move the three animals. Since I currently hold the *permiso*, I was tapped for the job. When I refused, Rivas volunteered. He has enough muscle and intelligence to carry it out."

"There must be *something* you can do to stop this. That snake is still nothing more than your servant."

"I am too old. Besides, I cannot risk the *permiso* going to Baja-Cruz. Everything I have worked for would have been in vain if that happened. They have no soul. Greed is all they're about. They will exploit this country and run it to the ground until we are all slaves of the North."

"Then you are a fool and a traitor. Do you think Rivas will do differently? Do you think he has the best interests of our people in mind? If Baja-Cruz is awarded the *permiso*, at least you know that you had no control over the consequences. By allowing Rivas to move forward with this travesty, you might as well put the gun to Juárez's head yourself."

"You are wise beyond your years, Xiomara. This was

decided long ago. I am too old, and Rivas knows it. They all know it. New times require new blood in this game. I am the last of a dying breed. At least, this way we will be allowed to live out our days in comfort and peace."

"Then all you said, all you supposedly believe in, is shit. All that matters to you is dying in a warm bed with food in your guts. I want no part of it."

As I turned away, he clutched my arm and yanked me toward him. "Don't be stupid!" he said. Even in the fading light, I could see the desperation in his eyes. "This is all beyond you, me, Rivas, and Baja-Cruz. It's even beyond the man who sits in the presidential palace today. We are not dealing with people here, we're not even dealing with laws or money. This is generations, centuries of spawning and nurturing a beast that transcends time and awareness, a beast that is at the core of our being, of what we think and believe and do. This beast must be fed with souls and blood like the gods of our ancestors. It is us, you and me. It is the children playing marbles in the street and the university professors and the housewives and the man who pumps the gas and lays down the highways. It is the market vendor and the pollution and the flag we salute every day. It is what we have become. How can we defeat what we are? We can dream and pray that things will change. We can chant the names of men like Juárez, who most certainly believe that things can be different, but that will never happen. We will never let that happen as much as we want to. Our actions from this point forward will determine whether we live or die. And maybe that would be a fair tradeoff, your life and mine for the life of Benigno Juárez. But it will be for nothing, and it won't just be me and you. Many others will share the same fate."

Once more I saw the fire in his eyes that had captivated me the first time we had met. I knew he spoke the truth. And yet it all felt so futile and meaningless, surrendering to men like Rivas and those who pulled his strings, and then sitting back and watching it all unfold.

Carlos disappeared for several weeks, leaving me alone in the house once again. I had asked him to take me along, because I did not want to be alone, not with the death of my parents so fresh in my mind. He refused, promising to take me to Europe when he returned from his business trip. He left behind a man to watch over me who identified himself only as The Spider. A balding, five-foot, four-inch abbreviation of a man, he was, according to Carlos, one of the most feared and admired security specialists in the western hemisphere, a one-man army who could kill and save a life with equal deft. Unlike Rivas, who was a sanguine, brutish warlord, The Spider was considered an artist, a craftsman in the clandestine game.

In the mornings he taught me basic self-defense techniques against hand, knife, and gun attacks. He demonstrated how not only to thwart an attacker, but also how to retaliate with a counter-attack and disarm him. After lunch he would take me to the shooting range outside the grounds of the estate and instruct me on how to load and shoot a Sako rifle and a Sig Sauer 9-mm handgun. He wrung into me the method for judging the location of a sniper, calculating the time interval between the crack of the bullet and the blast of the rifle or pistol, an interval between crack and blast that is one second long, for example, indicating a distance of 630 meters. He showed me how to adjust for wind velocity when targeting a shot by tying a cloth to a tree or mast and measuring the angle that the cloth assumed. We studied defensive formations used to counter an assassin's scope, such as the 360-degree formation in which a six-man squadron of bodyguards protects a client by surrounding him with each individual having the responsibility of securing a 180-degree area from which a kill shot might originate. The most effective, he claimed, was the spearhead formation, in which fourteen bodyguards form three lines that converge on the lead, or point man, forming an arrowhead or spear shape behind whom the potential target is positioned.

Our teacher-pupil relationship gradually evolved into a more personal one. He marveled at my dedication to the tasks he laid out for me, and I was grateful for his patience and moral support. I could tell that underneath his wrought-iron exterior he was a kind, humble man who had elected his profession out of necessity rather than by choice. His name was Pablo, and he had once been the martial arts instructor for the Cuban federal army. My training, he revealed, would be the last duty he would perform for Carlos, who, before leaving on his latest trip, had informed him that his services would no longer be required. He was hoping to return to Cuba under an assumed identity and reunite with the remaining members of his family.

One day after we had finished a shooting lesson, he turned to me, extending a cautious hand. "My condolences on the death of your parents," he said shyly.

"Thank you," I said, a bit taken aback by his forwardness.

"I lost my wife and daughter a long time ago," he said. "They were executed in front of me by a government-sponsored death squad sent out to stop an insurrection against the state. That was why I left Cuba. Everything there reminded me of my family and their end. I came here with the help of a reporter for *El Liberador* who lives in El Paso. His name is Abraham Spanich. He has many connections in and outside the country and is a good resource if you are ever in trouble."

In those days I would watch the news on television and read in the newspapers about the murders, the disappearances, the shootings, the drug shipments, and the corrupt government leaders. They were crimes assumed to have been perpetrated by unseen faces, rogue criminal factions, street gangs, paramilitary guerillas. I could not help but wonder what hand my beloved husband and his

henchman had played in all of this. I began to understand
what Carlos had meant when he told me about Juárez's
planned assassination. We were all playing a role in the
chaos; those of us who believed what we were told and
never questioned the source of the information and never
dared to look beyond the pixelated images of the blood
and the weeping mothers and the unidentified cadavers.
We were just as guilty as the ones who had done the
killing, the robbing, and the raping.

Was it any wonder that we were the pariah country of
the continent, the North's dysfunctional ward, the dirty
little secret that had to be both reprimanded for and protected from our own inequalities lest we smudge Big
Brother's image by association? But we still had our pride,
our belief that things could be better, that, naively or not,
we were the victims of circumstances and treachery, of our
overzealous desire to achieve what was on the other side
of the river and the barbed wire.

Carlos returned a month later looking more worn and
frail than I had ever seen him. The buoyancy in his eyes
had been anchored, and there was a hitch in his walk, as
if he were hiding a limp. He looked defeated and sad,
almost sick.

"It's happened," he told me after dinner. "The *permiso*
has been offered to Rivas, provided, of course, that he fol-
lows through with the Juárez business and . . ."

"What?"

"He must also do something to appease the North so
that they will not punish us by cutting off aid."

"What?"

"Offer a sacrifice."

"Who?"

"One of his own."

"Betray his own people?"

"The North wants proof that this government is doing
all it can to stop the flow of drugs into their country.

Arrests will be staged, mostly small-time runners, leading up to the capture of someone significant, not enough to really matter, but someone who will look good in a headline or a news report, along with a sizeable amount of product, of course. The North is not naïve enough to believe that we are actually surrendering an asset, but they do have people to appease. As long as their constituents are satisfied and the money continues to flow, nothing will really change."

"What will happen to you, to us?"

"We become other people."

In the days that followed, a series of drug arrests and seizures made the news. Carlos seemed more nervous than before and began to do something I had never seen him do: lace his cigarettes with cocaine. He didn't sleep, but was on the telephone around the clock talking mostly in German or French. From the few words that I was able to understand, I deduced that he was talking with financial representatives from the various institutions that guarded his money. He later disclosed to me that he had closed most of his foreign accounts except for two, one under his name in an undisclosed location, another in El Paso that was in my name, but that I could only access it in person after my identity had been verified through my fingerprints.

When I first heard about the assassination of Benigno Juárez on a radio broadcast, a perverse, childish sort of impulse made me want to laugh. It was like watching a magic trick and knowing the secret, but still marveling at its efficiency and masterful execution. He had been gunned down during the half-time festivities at a charity soccer match as he delivered a speech to more than a hundred thousand fans. The sniper's bullet had shattered his head and proceeded through the throat of Juárez's wife, who was standing directly behind him. A former fieldworker and expatriate who had recently returned from the north was being held and charged with the murder.

For several weeks, the nation was in mourning over the death of their son, the would-be savior of a nation under duress. There were candlelight vigils, riots, looting, accusations hurled toward the ruling party by those who saw the murder as a way for the political incumbents to ensure that they would retain control of the nation's most powerful political seat. Not even the North escaped implication, as it was felt by many that Benigno Juárez, a seemingly righteous, proud leader, threatened the North's role as economic and political curator of that corner of the globe.

I was awakened one day by a stillness, a profound void of activity that I sensed all around me. The house, I discovered, was empty. All of the servants and guards were gone, as was Carlos. I considered that perhaps I had not awakened and was, in fact, dreaming, for nothing so surreal was possible in a coherent state of awareness. That all-too-familiar voice proved otherwise.

"I cannot help but marvel at the delicious irony of life," said Rivas. "It is perhaps what makes it worth living."

He was standing on the green overlooking the back section of the estate, hands in his pockets, gaze fixed on nothing, like a man contemplating impending death or immortality.

"What are you doing here?"

"I've come for you, Xiomara. Now that we no longer have that nuisance of a marriage between you and Carlos to impede us, I thought it might be a good time to become reacquainted."

"Where is Carlos?"

"He's been called away on business. I'm afraid he may not return."

"Carlos no longer has business to take care of, not that kind, anyway. Besides, it appears that you're taking care of the business these days, or at least the part of it that suits you best."

"He must have told you about our little arrangement. Senile, old fool. I hope I am put out of my misery long before I become such a poor representative of human existence."

"You accomplished that long ago."

"I forgot how charming you are, Xiomara. It's one of the many qualities that drew me here to find you and propose that you annul your marriage to Carlos and become mine."

"You're insane."

"On the contrary, I've never enjoyed such clarity. You are a smart woman. If he told you about the stadium business, he must have told you everything else. He must have laid it all out for you, the reality of what life will be like from now on, now that I give the orders."

"I prefer death."

"One of my men is pointing to the back of your head with a laser that can only be seen with infrared goggles. If you've been watching television, you know he is a very good marksman. All I have to do is take one step to the left and life will go on for everyone except you. A step to the right and you, my marksman, and I will go have breakfast."

At that moment, everything Marina had told me about why she had taken the fetus from my womb made sense. Anything even remotely connected to the man—if indeed one could call him that—was an abomination that deserved nothing less than the swiftest, most complete erasure from this world.

"I will go with you, but I must visit my parents' graves one last time," I said.

"Of course," he said, smiling that smile I had grown to loathe.

One of Rivas' men, presumably the one who had been ready to put a bullet through my head, escorted me to the Ave Blanca cemetery that evening. He was tall, firmly built, and smelled like old, sweat-hardened clothes. He did not speak and only acknowledged my presence by mimicking every move I made. He would never come closer to me than arm's length and would not walk next to me or directly behind me. The Spider had told me that this was the trick of an old pro, of someone used to setting up hits or being the target of them.

As I finished paying my respects at the grave site, I stood motionless, knowing he would wait until I moved, but hoping he would lose his patience and advance toward me. I figured such a roughly honed man would be ready for anything, but my advantage was a sizeable one. No one, I firmly believed, would have expected what I was planning, not from a woman.

At last I heard his footsteps approaching. I waited just as The Spider had taught me, trying to sense the direction from which the attack would come. The moment I felt his left hand on my right shoulder, I clamped it with my left hand while simultaneously stepping back with my right foot and back-fisting the bridge of his nose. This stunned him momentarily. Before he could recover, I lowered my right hand and hammer-fisted him in the groin, driving his upper body forward. As he leaned into me, I raised my right elbow and drove it into his chin, turning instantly and impaling his exposed throat with my index and middle knuckles. He immediately dropped to the ground, clutching his neck and gasping for air. I had felt his windpipe give and knew that he would be incapacitated for a while, choking on his own blood. Not waiting to find out, I drove away from Ave Blanca in the bodyguard's rusted Volkswagen, trying to retrace the route the bus had taken when I had fled The Orchid and blessing the day I had met the man they called The Spider.

I found Marina out on the beach chasing hermit crabs. "I've been expecting you," she said. "Now that my brother is gone, you're all I have."

"Where is he?" I pleaded, still incredulous that the

man who only months before could have ruled the world had been the victim of the ultimate coup détat.

"Probably dead," she said, picking sand from between her fingers. "And if he isn't, he might as well be."

"It was Rivas."

"I know."

"He will kill me, too."

"He will not seek you here, even if he suspects this is where you have come."

"How do you know?"

"His fear of me is too great."

I recounted to Marina all that had happened since Carlos had told me about the plans for Juárez's assassination. She nodded and patted the back of my hand. "You must leave here," she said finally.

"No," I pleaded. "If he will not come here, why would I ever want to leave?"

"Because if you don't leave, Xiomara, you will end up like me, and there is so much waiting for you."

"But the moment I leave here I will be at his mercy. I won't live out a day."

"Xiomara, that is why you must hurry. It will take him a day or two to figure out where you are. He is a powerful man, but he knows of my own power and will not take action hastily. He'll try to wait you out. You must go into town. There is a telephone in the central market. You must call the reporter and tell him your story. He will find a way to get you out of here."

"You have foreseen this?"

"Destiny is a cruel trickster. It sometimes shows us the good, so when it comes to pass, we are undying believers in its word. It is then that it shows us the bad, but by then we are so blinded by our delusion, as Rivas is, that we neglect to remember that with destiny there is always two outcomes. Whether it is good or bad depends on us. I have foreseen the destiny that culminates in your death.

The other destiny is to be written by you, should you choose to do so."

Even at 8:00 a.m., the line of people waiting to use the town's only telephone wound almost completely around the building that housed the central market. At the rate that the line was advancing, I calculated that it would take most of the day for me to get my turn at the telephone, and I still needed to figure out how I was going to find Spanich. I only had the name of the newspaper where he worked, and I had heard from several of the other people in line that the telephone would only allow outgoing collect calls.

The market closed with the phone booth still nowhere in sight. Some of the people ahead of me went home. Most of them slumped onto the rocky street, unwrapping tacos they had brought, or going to sleep. As I ate the roasted chicken Marina had packed for me, I caught sight of the wedding ring that was still balanced on my finger. Carlos had custom-ordered it from Italy; the twenty-four-carat gold band alone was worth thousands.

"This for one phone call?" said the sleepy market owner, who weighed the ring in his hand as he wiped remnants of his supper from his teeth with his tongue.

"One phone call of unspecified length," I clarified.

"Collect?"

"Of course."

There was no answer at the offices of *El Liberador*, even after the operator tried a third time. She presumed that they were closed and suggested that I try in the morning. Indignant, she agreed to try the residential listing for Spanich. "Tell him The Spider is calling," I insisted as a groggy, irritated voice answered at the other end of the line.

"Who?" There was silence for a few seconds, then: "I will accept the call."

He was surprised when he heard a woman's voice on

the other end of the line and almost hung up, but I managed to persuade him otherwise after revealing who I was—or had been—and that I had information involving the Arquimedes-Savón cartel and the northern government. He told me that we should not talk on the telephone, that it was too dangerous for me to stay on the street. I told him I was scared and had but a few hundred pesos, but that I had access to large amounts of money if I could get to El Paso. He said he had contacts at the U.S. State Department who might grant me amnesty in exchange for my information, if it was significant enough. I told him it was unprecedented, and he suggested that I hire a taxi to take me to Chihuahua as soon as possible. The taxi would not be restricted to the main highways where check stations were set up every few hundred kilometers. Traveling any farther north without detection would be impossible. Once in Chihuahua, I was to locate a man named Alto McKim, manager of a nightclub called El Pajarín. He would put me in contact with a smuggler named Nando Flores, who would transport me to Ciudad Juárez. There I would rendezvous with him.

As I walked toward the edge of town in the direction of The Orchid, I caught sight of a shiny black Suburban with tinted windows slowly creeping onto the town's main thoroughfare. There was no mistaking its origin or its intentions. I realized that even in the thickening darkness, I was as conspicuous as the Suburban and would be easily spotted, so I ducked into a patio of one of the houses that lined the streets and exchanged my jeans and blouse for a sun-bleached cotton dress. I circumvented the Suburban and headed back to the hacienda, where I hoped to convince Marina to accompany me to Chihuahua.

I knew something was wrong when I smelled the burned beans. Marina had once explained that allowing the beans to burn was one of a woman's greatest failings, that it not only proved she was a bad cook, but also signified that she was not fit to be the caretaker of a home. Although I had scoffed at such a belief, I learned to understand how this trivial ideal was so firmly embedded in a society that had yet to accept the notion that women could prove their worth outside the kitchen.

The pot of beans that would have accompanied the main course of the three meals the following day had actually been spilled over the gas burners and across the floor. The half-kneaded dough that Marina would have shaped into tortillas lay smattered in clumps across the counter and walls. I found the old woman in the patio, barely breathing.

"He came," she said with disbelief when I lifted her face out of the dirt, the dough still clinging to her fingers and hair. I could see a small hole just below her left shoulder where a bullet had entered. On the other side of her body, however, there was a crater of blood and bone. She was practically lifeless as I brushed the dirt from her face. Her eyes rolled in their sockets, but they reflected no light, no energy, no presence of a human essence. She was dying.

"You must leave," the strained voice said. "Go to the water."

"I got a hold of Spanich. He told me to go to El Paso to meet him. I want you to come with me."

"I am going with you," she said. "We all are."

I saw her eyes flutter one last time and then she was gone. For a moment I felt as if I were staring down at my mother's body. There was no pain or sorrow, but a sense of connection with both of them. I remembered something Marina had once told me about her belief in the afterlife. She said that when we die, we become part of a collective, an omniscient awareness that allows us to be whatever and whomever we choose. As I walked to the beach through the jungle, I felt them all around me: in the trees, the flowers, the birds, the air, on the ground, in the sky, and in the surging waves on which Marina's small canoe bobbed patiently against a horizon of mist and twilight.

Exodus

Night had fallen as Nando awoke shivering in the cold, stale air, the moldy odor of vinyl and plastic clogging his nostrils. He wiped his sleep-encrusted eyes and saw that someone was in the car with him. He stared at Xiomara's seemingly lifeless body, amazed by how young she looked, just a little girl taking a nap while she waited for her mother to return from the market.

The premature loss of innocence was commonplace in a society that sent boys, barely old enough to feed themselves, to the fields or the street corners, and girls, considered undesirable and forgotten if they did not marry by the time they were twenty, to lonely altars. His own mother had been married at thirteen to his father, a seventeen-year-old farmhand with dreams of one day owning land himself.

The desperation clung to Xiomara as awkwardly as the handmade dress she wore. He wondered if it was as obvious on him. Desperation could be dangerous. But perhaps his years of waxing deception had paid off, for she had yet to exhibit the seductive smile of someone getting ready to fuck him over. Perhaps she had told him the truth about the job, after all.

Nando decided to let her sleep while he looked the car over, fully expecting the slamming doors and the crunch of the hood after he had checked the fluids and cables to awaken her. Rather than awaken her, the noise seemed to have a reassuring effect, and she sank deeper into the kind of sleep that is perhaps a heartbeat or two away from death. By the time he was maneuvering the car out of the city and toward the dark mountains, she was snoring like a man. It made him smile.

"Where are we?" Xiomara said in a voice that was still milky with sleep. "Why is it so dark?"

"Headed for the Devil's Horns," Nando answered, only slightly cognizant of the fact that she was not from the area and had probably never heard of such a place.

"Do you mean that metaphorically?" she said, a bit more clear-headed.

"Geographically. It's what the locals call the pass on the Cumbre Mountains. We should be there in forty-five minutes or so."

"So we are in the mountains?" she said, amused.

"Yes, ten thousand five hundred feet, to be exact."

"I've never been in the mountains," she said, gazing out the window, although the most she could have possibly seen in the dark were the few straggly mesquite shrubs that lined the brittle road. "I never thought it would be like this. Even the air tastes different."

"I would think that there isn't much a person like you hasn't seen or done."

"When your veins are full of heroin, everything is artificial and diluted. You might as well be dead because nothing you experience is real. It's like I've been in a coma or having an out-of-body experience for the past two years."

"Your ears are going to start feeling funny."

"Funny?"

"Like they are going to burst."

"My God, why didn't you tell me—?"

"Just yawn."

"What?"

"Yawn. You'll be all right."

Xiomara was quiet then, as if she were trying to dissect the logic of what he had just said. A few minutes later she said, "It worked."

The road had become treacherous now, and Nando worried that the rimless tires of the corroded Riviera would not hold out. It would not have mattered had they been riding in a Land Rover fresh off the assembly line. The rocks here were so dense and so sharp, they could slice through tires, grilles, bumpers. He remembered the time he had been stranded after a jagged rock had punctured the gas tank on an old Chevette with a bad muffler and a broken heater that he had tried to transport. It had taken him an entire day and part of the night to reach the outskirts of Chihuahua, lucky to have suffered only moderate dehydration and a minor case of frostbite in his toes.

"Do you think we'll see snow?" she said, bright-eyed with anticipation. Just a child, he thought again, recognizing a charming sort of naïveté.

"Too early for snow, maybe a little frost."

"You think I'm foolish?"

"I've just never met anyone who is so taken aback by . . . mountains."

"There aren't many where I am from, not this high. The ones that do exist are too far away, so we just don't bother with them."

"You're from the provinces, Xiomara?"

"Not that far south."

He waited for her to elaborate, finding that the sound of her voice was calming his apprehension. Maybe that was what had been missing during his desert treks, a companion, someone to ride out the loneliness with him. But there was no response, and when he looked at her again, she no longer reminded him of a child. She was the same desperate woman he had found hunched over a table at El Pajarín.

"Nando, are you tired?" she asked finally.

"In my line of work that's not an option. Besides, I have this, just in case." He reached over and popped the glove compartment.

"What is it?" she said.

"Hot sauce. I took it from the club."

"What's it for?"

"If I start to get tired, I suck a little bit of it."

Xiomara began to laugh. Nando soon realized that he, too, was laughing, and it felt like the most natural thing in the world. Their laughter seemed to envelop them in a veil of innocence.

There was a knock underneath the car. They froze. He nudged the car to a halt, placing a finger to his lips, his hand aching for the familiar oily grip of his .38 revolver, which, he remembered with a plume of panic, was gone. He waited. His eyes flashed side to side, to the roof of the car, to the darkness outside the window, to his feet, then to the girl.

"Is your door locked?" he whispered.

She nodded. "What's wrong?" she mouthed.

"We're here," he said after a prolonged silence.

"Where?"

"The Devil's Horns. Eleven thousand feet above sea level."

"What was that sound?"

"Probably just a rock, but you can never be sure. This is where they like to wait."

"Who?"

"Bandits, reversers, anybody crazy enough to try to take down a transport."

"Who uses these back roads?"

"Farmers, Tarahumara Indians, people like me."

"Are you scared?

"I've been scared for ten years."

They began to move again. The sharp descent was immediately noticeable. What he failed to tell her was that it didn't matter if he was scared or not, or if he was armed. If somebody was waiting to take them down at that particular location, there would be nothing they could do.

There would be no way they could defend themselves. Even if they tried to make a break for it in the car, they would not get far before slamming into one side of the mountain or plunging down the other.

"Is that how long you've been doing this?" she asked.

"Not quite that long," Nando answered, intrigued and slightly annoyed that she was unwilling to reveal anything about herself yet was eager to know about him. He didn't care. It wasn't as if he would be running for office anytime soon.

"Before this I was a *pollero*. You probably know them as *coyotes*. I used to smuggle people across the border. Before that I was a chauffeur for prostitutes. Before that I sold fake green cards to immigrants and illegal cigars to tourists."

"Oh," she said, clearly embarrassed by her inquiry.

Just when he thought their conversation had ended, Xiomara said, "If they catch us, they'll kill us. You know that, don't you?"

"I would be an idiot to think otherwise."

"Why did you agree to help me?"

"I need the money."

They arrived at an old tire-repair shop at the entrance of Villa Oscura, in the predawn hours, when it seems the earth is holding its breath. Exhausted, Nando had fallen asleep even before the engine had finished ticking to its death. Xiomara, who had drifted back to sleep shortly after leaving the Devil's Horns, was still snoring away in the backseat. And she was shivering in her sleep. Although it was late summer and the town was situated a few thousand feet below the Cumbre Mountains, a damp chill hung about the moldy walls of the broken-down shop.

Nando removed his denim jacket and draped it over her shoulders. She seemed to relax, nudging her head deeper into the plush of the seat. There was a magnetism about her, a stifled charge that flowed off her brow and the nape of her neck, down to her knees and ankles. He felt a need to touch her then, to rub her cheek or stroke her hair or cradle her legs, but he somehow sensed that if he indulged his impulses, the consequences would be dire.

The morning bloomed in an expulsion of fast, buoyant light leaving no trace of the previous night's dreariness. Nando drank in the scent of burning wood. A hundred souls preparing for another day. He could smell it all, the coffee and the pinto beans, the eggs with *chorizo*, the sweet bread, the freshly ground salsa, and, of course, the tortillas. It was breakfast time in Villa Oscura.

The road that had led them down the mountain intersected at the north end of town with one of the main highways that linked to Ciudad Juárez. The repair shop was adjacent to the mountain road behind an abandoned bus terminal that had been transformed into the First Catholic Church of Villa Oscura. Tokyo had thought it a good omen for the shed to be situated next to such a pious establishment. It was Tokyo's shed. No question about it whatsoever. He had purchased it from a mechanic tired of a drab, uneventful rural life and eager to bestow his automotive expertise upon the good people of Juárez. It had saved his transport, not to mention his ass, on more than one occasion, particularly the time when the Transportation Authority had issued a contract for his capture.

Tokyo had planned to turn the shed into a veritable fort, installing state-of-the-art fuel pumps, a GPS system, an underground bunker with caches of food, water, and weapons, and, eventually, a tunnel large enough to run automobiles through. So far, he had managed to stock it with a few five-gallon cans of gasoline and one of those fake spare tires that make a car look crippled, all of which he had buried in a metal drum near the back wall.

The toy tire was gone, as was most of the gasoline. Good old reliable Tokyo. Nando emptied what was left in two gas cans into the Buick, coaxing the fuel gauge just over a quarter tank. There was no way he would be able to score the additional fuel they would need in Villa Oscura, a town that ran mostly on horsepower, literally. They would be cutting it close. They would probably have to walk the last ten miles into Juárez.

He thought about waking her, but didn't want to disturb what must have been the best sleep she had had in days, or longer. He figured she would be out for at least another hour, plenty of time for him to run into town and bring back breakfast. Even if she had been awake, he would have insisted that she stay put. Evasion and escape were always more feasible when there was no one else to worry about but himself.

Nando had not eaten in almost two days, and he doubted that the girl had fared much better. What he wouldn't do for a plate of *huevos rancheros* with home-made *pico de gallo* or a bowl of *posole* with diced cabbage, onions, and lime juice. He was certain to find both in Villa Oscura. There was, however, one problem. He was broke, and, by all accounts, she was as well. There was nothing more pitiful than the broke and the hungry. Well, perhaps the broke, the hungry, and the short on fuel. It was then that he saw the stack of empty soda bottles in a corner of the shed. Good old reliable Tokyo.

The streets of Villa Oscura were narrow paths speckled with rough, mossy stones on which the balding tires of the few automobiles—delivery trucks and buses mostly—that occasionally meandered through town could purchase traction. The sparse clay and cracked cinderblock buildings lining the streets drooped precariously under the weight of their own solitude. Stray dogs and patio hens scoured the muddy edges of the buildings for food scraps or a cool worm. Shawl-covered women carrying towering stacks of tortillas that drove his salivary glands into a frenzy filled the crowded doorways of the mill and meat market. Except for a store clerk, an ice-cream vendor, and an aging porch sitter, most of the townsmen had taken to the fields or to the mountains to do their daily work. It was for this reason, he guessed, that he managed to provoke the indicting stares of the dutiful wives, sisters, and daughters that were Villa Oscura's only inhabitants for the better part of the day. It didn't help that he was lugging two cartons of empty soda bottles under each arm. Still, such isolated communities cherished their privacy and normally bridled their curiosity.

Panadería Central, a small, dough-colored mercantile that generated the alternating scents of freshly baked bread and grilled beef that could be detected from blocks away, was the hub of the town's activity. There was a glint of recognition in the clerk's eyes as he walked in, nodding politely at the dozen or so patrons who were crammed ahead of him.

He ordered a dozen corn tortillas, a pound of eggs and *chorizo*, and two cups of coffee. The clerk seemed annoyed at his currency, but accepted the bottles and even gave him twenty pesos in change, which he used to buy three Patito pastries and a Pelón lollipop that sprouted *tamarindo*-flavored hair when you pressed the rubber-coated top shaped like a boy's head. He bundled the food into an old plastic bag the clerk offered him, securing a cup of coffee in each hand, and headed back to the repair shop.

He found Xiomara squatting in a corner of the shed and immediately turned his head in embarrassment. "I've brought you some food," he said.

"Thank you," she said, readjusting her clothes. "I didn't mean to be disrespectful. I was just afraid to go outside."

He waved off her apology, still evading her gaze.

"Is that coffee I smell?" she said, the smile painting her voice.

"I found some old bottles and traded them for breakfast," he said, emptying the plastic bag on the hood of the car.

"For me?" she said, taking one of the Patito pastries.

"This, too," he said, handing her the Pelón lollipop.

"These were my favorite when I was a little girl," she said.

For the first time Nando saw the lovely emerald shimmer of her eyes head on. It was like staring into the steely challenge of a hawk, devoid of everything except the wildest, most pristine beauty. It was truth.

"I've never met a girl who didn't like Pelones," he said.

The coffee was strong and sweet and reminded him of home and his mother who had always assured him that little boys who drank coffee grew ears like those on a donkey. He had started drinking coffee when he was six years old, despite his mother's scolding. It had been her own fault. Her coffee had been so sweet—he preferred it to candy or soda—and there wasn't a thing he looked forward to more every morning than sneaking a few sips of it as it simmered on the stove. Eventually, his mother relented and even molded for him his own clay cup. She had decorated it with a cartoon-like sketch of a donkey with long, pointed ears.

Nando took out The Chart, as he affectionately referred to the top flap of a grapefruit box that he used to trace all of his routes through the territories surrounding Juárez, and studied the fading network of lines on the disintegrating cardboard. He'd have to darken them when he got back. It was a work in progress, and he planned to one day transfer it to a more durable and legible format. Hell, he could probably peddle it on street corners in Juárez and El Paso. The Smuggler's Guide, he would call it. All the routes were color-coded. Black was for a small transport, two to five cars. Blue was for larger, more volatile shipments, guns or explosives. He had once delivered a recreational vehicle crammed with crates of Gaboon Vipers, East Asian cobras, and South Saharan scorpions. The red route he had used only on two occasions, once to deliver a batch of vials that contained some form of exotic virus that had been stolen from a lab up north. The other instance he had hauled a trailer carrying three prize-winning thoroughbreds that had been snatched from a derby in California. This time, however, he felt he needed a special route, one he had never used before, one that didn't exist. With the tip of a plain lead pencil that he had found on the floorboard of the Riviera, he began to trace a wandering, gray route from Villa Oscura to the Ciudad Juárez landfill.

They ate in silence, devouring each bite with animalistic ferocity and savoring as if it were their last. His thoughts inevitably skipped back to his family and his childhood. The hunger that had been tearing at his gut reminded him of those destitute times when his mother had been unable to feed herself or her children.

Nando had been born the last of seven children. Benicio, his father, had been a drunk, and his mother sold cosmetics and rented out one of the rooms of their three-bedroom house to students from the local technical college, so eight of them, counting his mother, shared the other two rooms. Benicio almost never came home, and when he managed to sober up enough to be able to walk out of the local cantina, he stopped by only for a couple of hours, and those he mostly spent yelling at Nando's mother. He eventually stopped coming altogether.

In the fifteen years that he lived at home, Nando could never remember times being anything but hard, often unbearably hard when there was no food at all in the house. His brothers and sisters all worked part-time jobs to help out with the bills. But one by one they began to leave, establishing their own lives, their own families, eventually losing touch with each other. Who could blame them? Before too long it was just his mother, his oldest brother Serafín and he. Even with just two of them to take care of, the strain soon took its toll on Serafín, and he was soon following in Benicio's footsteps. It only got worse when their mother's diabetic condition deteriorated.

After her funeral, Serafín plunged into a seemingly bottomless depression, and living with him became purgatory. In his drunken rages he would accuse Nando of being an illiterate, a lazy vagrant, a homosexual. It became customary for him to take out the shotgun he had gotten as a birthday gift from their grandfather years earlier and inch it up to his own chin. The occasion when he had actually pulled the trigger was the one time he had forgotten to load the goddamned thing. Nando soon realized that it would be better for both of them if he left Serafín alone with his demons. And he did, sneaking out one morning while his brother slept off a night of drinking that had ended with every piece of furniture, wall fixture, and decoration in the house destroyed.

Nando settled in Ciudad Juárez, gateway to the mythical North, land of fancy coffee shops, minimum wage, and Disneyland. He had been living there for less than a month, and already he was desperate. Work was scarce, and the only jobs available involved either hauling contraband across the border or hawking it to the tourists. Cuban cigars were in vogue, especially among the college kids, but the supplier took most of what he made, leaving him with barely enough for his daily staple of two *carne asada* tacos and a bottle of Carta Blanca that he devoured as he walked back to the rotting wooden shed he shared with three indentured servants from Costa Rica. He moonlighted as a carrier for a pharmacist who fabricated resident cards that he sold from his back office for two hundred dollars a pop. He would drop them off at a *torta* stand a couple of blocks from the Chamizal bridge. A majority of the prospective crossers were farmers from the provinces with only enough money to pay the *pollero* for passage to the other side. Attempting to walk across the bridge into the United States with one of these fake cards in hand was inconceivable, since the border guards could spot a fake card in an instant. The idea was to get across illegally and use the cards as work permits, considering that in those days, few people outside the field of law enforcement would even know what a resident card looked like. The pharmacist was lucky to sell three of them in a month's time.

"You're in the wrong business, *mojado*," said a gaunt redhead with twin ear hoops and a goatee. Nando had seen the guy around town herding the local street talent and always figured him for a pimp.

"What's it to you?"

"A resourceful young man like yourself should put his talents to better use."

"What do you know of my talents?"

"I've been studying you, the way you deal with customers, the way they let their guard down around you. You have the talent making people trust you, and that carries great potential in this city. Cigar peddling is for the snot-nosed Tarahumara kids running around here like mice. You ever want to make some real money, you come down to the Tres Palmas Hotel and ask for Chango." Then he was gone like an hallucination.

Nando went down to the Tres Palmas the very next morning.

"You married?" she asked, nibbling on her third taco.

"No," Nando said, smiling sheepishly.

"There must be someone praying that you get back in one piece."

"I wouldn't do that to anyone."

"Nobody? Ever?"

"A long time ago."

"You loved her?"

"Very much."

"But it wasn't enough?"

"We were at different crossroads in our lives."

The wounds were still as raw as the day she had kicked him to the curb. She was a resplendent gem of a woman, with blond hair, peach-colored eyes, and a radiant smile. She had come to Mexico as a volunteer with one of the churches from the North. Her group would gather at the *zócalo* every Sunday morning to preach, play the guitar, and pass out blankets, hot chocolate (the packets of dirt-colored powder that always gave him diarrhea), and graham crackers. He had always found them annoying with their loud, insistent voices, their undaunted cheeriness and sweet-smelling clothes. But the prospect of scoring a blanket or two, maybe a pair of shoes or some of those strange, dried noodles that suddenly became edible with just a cup of boiling water—all of which could turn a hefty profit at one of the open-air markets downtown—was worth suffering through the religious sideshow.

She had been standing in the middle of a group of confused women, trying to explain the mechanics of a small tube-shaped wad of paper with a string attached to one end of it. They were popular with the gutter punks who doused them with *toncho* and tied them around their necks for quick and easy access to their chemically singed nostrils. Watching her charm the women with her broad, slightly embarrassed smile—and the most perfect white teeth he had ever seen—made him smile, too, although he must have looked like some mentally idle mouth breather standing there in the middle of the crowded *zócalo* grinning like he had just crapped his pants.

"Jesus loves you," she said as Nando stepped up to her, still brandishing that idiotic smile.

Then it was a smiling contest between the two of them. She must have certainly been paralyzed by the presence of this dark-haired, sun-scorched sweaty mestizo. He, on the other hand, had discovered the captive magnificence of her eyes, whose color and luster defied his vocabulary.

A week later, he was an honorary member of the Vineyard Christian Fellowship of God, passing out pamphlets sooty with ink and tabloid-like mini-magazines with headlines that declared "Rejoice!" or "In His Words" or "Divine Kingdom Awaits". The other volunteers, particularly the men, thought the latter assertion humorous for this street rat with a crush.

Her name was Mya. She was fluent in Spanish, but said her ancestors were German. Mya was not the least bit reluctant to engage him in linguistic games that he invented to break down his ignorance and her shyness. He would tell her jokes in Spanish, and recite sappy poems he composed for her after they parted company every Sunday.

Divina
Supieras las tormentas que causas dentro de mí.
No puedo parpadear sin sentir el aliento de tu mirada,
El calor de tu sonrisa.
Eres como un astro, un planeta
En el cielo oscuro de mis sueños
Por ti, todo.

When Nando had recited this, Mya's eyes flickered, floating across the words he had scrawled on a dirty piece of notebook paper. Then she looked up and around her, bewildered as if she had forgotten where she was or how she had gotten there. Holding her hand to her chest, she would begin to cry. He felt ashamed that he had coaxed her out there to that poor excuse of a city zoo on a day that she would have otherwise been shopping at a mall or working in her garden. It was a two-hour bus ride from her home in Las Cruces, and not a very comfortable or safe one at that. The fact that she had agreed to come, defying the rules of her congregation against fraternizing with the natives, especially of the opposite sex, and negating her own common sense, had led him to the conclusion that she had developed the same feelings toward him that he was feeling toward her.

Wiping the tears from her cheeks, Mya at last began to smile, and Nando began to breathe again. Lifting her face up to his gaze, he told her that he loved her, that he had dreamt of her throughout his childhood and adolescence as he lay in that tiny bed that he and his siblings shared. He told her she was all he wanted, that with her by his side his life would be complete.

Mya stopped coming across the border with the church group, but instead waited for the weekends when she would arrive at the Juárez bus terminal carrying a gift or a souvenir from the North—a T-shirt, a pail of strawberries, or a stack of homemade egg rolls. He invited her to a dance one night and had to sneak across the border in order to meet her at the bus stop so that she did not have to ride into Juárez alone, with all the gangsters and thugs cruising the streets. She had laughed the entire night as she watched the sleepy trot that the couples were slinging with their hips and shoulders, mimicking the rhythm of *cumbias* and *merengues* and waltzes that the band was fusing.

During the intermissions Mya told him that she was divorced, that she hadn't seen anyone romantically for three years, and that she was studying to be a beautician. Nando told her he was a student at the local university. She asked him if he believed in God. He lied again and said that he did. He asked her if she could ever marry a Mexican. She said yes, but that her family would probably disown her if she did. Then they danced, and he brought her close to him, nestled his face into the cup of her ear and neck. Her skin was soft as flour and smelled of lemons and watermelon, and the rest of her seemed to dissolve into him, breasts against sternum, her belly meshing with his pelvis, her legs dovetailing in between his.

It was then that he understood the profundity of his love for her and how it seemed to rage like a windblown brush fire whenever her eyes flirted with his or when she shook her head and curled her mouth to dismiss something in a slightly flippant, disinterested way, or when she bit the right corner of her lower lip while pensive.

Nando traded Cano Moreno, a fifteen-year-old apprentice tattoo artist, the down payment on a resident card for a bit of his handiwork. *Por ti todo, Mya* read the scabbing, oozing welts on his abdomen, above them her likeness, duplicated from one of the photographs she had given him, emblazoned across his chest in thousands of miniscule ink perforations.

"I can't do this anymore," she had said the next time she came to see him. "We have to end this before we become involved in something we can neither understand nor control."

"But I thought we both wanted this. That we loved each other."

"I do love you, but . . ."

"But what?"

"We're too different. There's no way this can be anything more than a weekend diversion, a fantasy. It will destroy us."

"You mean I will destroy you."

"They wouldn't understand. They would never see you the way I see you."

"Your family?"

"Everyone who's close to me."

"Let's leave, go somewhere we can be alone together, where we don't have to justify our love or be second-guessed by anyone."

"You have no money, and I would have to give everything up, and, well, I'm not prepared to do that."

"Then you don't love me."

Mya stifled a sarcastic laugh and dropped her eyes the way she always did when she momentarily lost control. He found her face and pulled it close to his, hating the way she felt cold and artificial in his arms. With his lips he scooped the tears from her eyes and swallowed them. Then he turned and walked out of the bus terminal, his abdomen throbbing, his mouth salty, and his heart bleeding.

"I guess it's worse for a woman," said Xiomara.

"What is?" inquired Nando.

"Being alone. And it's not just being alone, it's the dirty little secret people always associate with it."

"I find it hard to believe that you have that problem."

"You'd be surprised. I was married once. I cheated on my husband."

"You were with the wrong man. I wouldn't call that cheating. I'd call it rebellion. You got pressured into marrying him, right?"

"Something like that."

"You're lucky."

"How so?"

"You reacted to the situation. And you're still young enough to try again."

The chill of early morning was quickly giving way to a debilitating heat. He had been watching her as they sat inches across from each other, the shine of perspiration on her neck, the outline of her breasts against the damp dress, the slight parting of her knees. He had inched toward her as they talked, finding it harder and harder to resist the temptation, the need to touch her, to feel the warmth of her body, the force of her pulse.

"You're beautiful," he said, lowering his hand onto her knee.

Her hand suddenly shot out in a back fist that raked him across the bridge of the nose. His eyes flooded with tears, and he could feel the blood start to trickle from one nostril.

"You have no right," she said, throwing the taco she had been eating at his feet. "So that's what this is about. You thought stinking coffee and a couple of greasy tacos were going to make me spread my legs for you."

"Forgive me," he said, tasting the blood on his upper lip. "I didn't mean to offend you. I just wanted you to know that I think you're beautiful."

"You're all alike," she snarled. "You think that because you find me attractive, that gives you the right to try to take advantage of me. You think my physical appearance is the sole basis for my worth, that it's all I have to offer. I'm not here to satisfy anybody or appease egos. I'm not a pet or a toy, or some damn fucking machine."

"Did you tell that to McKim?"

"I did what I had to do, and it's none of your business."

"At least he got his compensation up front."

"And you will get yours . . . I was beginning to respect you."

Xiomara stormed out of the shed, leaving Nando trembling with embarrassment and licking his upper lip. He could hear the town coming alive in the distance, semi trucks groaning along the nearby highway, dogs squealing, children yelping in a nearby school yard, the innocence crisp in their echoing laughter. He would have given anything to be that young again, to experience that innocence. Having dropped out of school to shine shoes in the crowded plazas of Delicias, he had never been much of a student, not for a lack of intelligence, but rather as a result of being possessed of a restless spirit.

Nando found her crouched up against the back of the shed, watching the morning mist recede into the western mountain range. He could already taste the heat that would gouge the afternoon. They would have to wait it out in the shed.

"Take this," he said, handing her one of the Patitos. "They're better if they've been in the freezer, but they're not bad warm."

"I'm not hungry anymore," she said, her words still brittle with rage.

"We should go back inside," he said, keeping a sizeable distance from her. The shame was making it difficult to talk. How could he express his regret to her, convey the overwhelming sensation of desperation and loneliness that were waging war inside his head? It had been ages since he had known the warmth of a woman, and for a moment he had forgotten common civility.

"Perhaps it was a mistake," she said, "thinking I could make this work."

"What I tried to do is unforgivable," he said. "I give you my word that nothing like that will happen again."

"You don't understand. It's not just that. It's everything. This trip, this crazy thing I'm trying to pull off. If it was just me, I think I'd be able to deal with it better, but now I've gotten you involved. Too many people have already suffered because of my childish whims, my impetuousness, my pride."

He was in awe of this unconventional young woman, her spirit and resolve unprecedented, that vigor in her voice, the impatient light that reflected from her eyes, telling the whole world that there wasn't anything she couldn't overcome.

"The man I told you about, Arquimedes-Savón . . . I was married to him. Actually, I still am. About a week ago I learned that there is a man in his organization who is going to betray him, have him killed or arrested to appease the North. The man's name is Rivas. When Rivas found out that Carlos had confided in me, he asked me to join him. I had no choice but to agree. Two days later I fled. An acquaintance told me about a reporter in El Paso who might be able to help me get out of the country, maybe put me in touch with people who would be interested in the information that I have. Not that I think it will make a difference, or maybe I do. I'm just tired."

"You hired me to take you to Juárez. I will do everything within my power to get you there. I know the kind of men you talk about, so I know the risks. There's no need for you to have my safety on your conscience."

"This man, Rivas, is not really a man. He is subhuman, a devil. He will hunt me, destroying anyone and anything that gets in his way. It's not just death we have to fear, it's what will come before, the atrocities."

The heat churned and swelled, invading the shed through every crevice, every crack, in the rotting wood. The town had wilted as its citizens performed the daily ritual of retreating into their homes in the hope of finding refuge during the two or three hours in the afternoon when the heat reached its zenith, tearing at one's body like a sickle. The only detectable sound was that of the heat itself, like some giant, languid reptile scouring its rough belly against the scorched earth.

Xiomara had gone back to sleep. She was like a cloth doll left in a rainstorm, discarded and soiled, living proof that even people with money had problems. Nando's memory began to filter through the dusty image of a small, round face with a smile as big as the horizon, ketchup-smeared lips, and a look that trembled with exhaustion and a dreamy terror of the coming night.

God, he wanted to get as far away from the border as possible, and he would if he could pull this off. It wasn't just the money. It was the spectrum of possibilities that would open up like a prism of light in a blind man's eyes: The beachfront cantina that served ice-cold beer from the only refrigerator for miles and the *ceviche* Serafín had taught him to prepare before his mind was eaten away by bitterness and anger. There was that old bitch of a Harley he'd brought in on his first job that he rescued after the buyer had crashed it into the side of a charter bus when he was a twelve pack and two bottles of Sauza past sanity. The driver had left it gathering dust, its front end mangled like some boxer's nose, in Tokyo's garage with neither the time nor the money to repair it. Best of all, there would be no more mile after desolate mile of desert road, the demons floating just beyond the reach of the headlamps, nothing to look forward to except another day of wondering how he had managed to make it that far.

Darkness had crept upon the city, and he could already see the night dwellers skirting the imperfect shadows of the decaying alleyways and street corners looking for prey, for someone like the frail, unsuspecting child who stood wearing hope on her tattered turquoise dress as she watched a group of children eating *banderillas*, Chihuahua's lumpy, oozing, dough-smothered rendition of a corn dog.

"What's your name?" he had asked.

"Luisa."

"Where do you live?"

"On top," she said, pointing to the mountain range just east of the city where he knew the majority of the Tarahumara Indian settlements were located. A once prosperous and self-sufficient people, they had lived off the land and raised their families in cherished isolation. Then the droughts had come, killing off their crops and livestock, forcing them to abandon their rustic utopia and venture into the cities below, where they lived as vagrants and were treated by the mestizos like some new breed of street vermin. Those who remained in the mountains were swept into a web of neo-slavery, an unyielding bondage to the narcos who had wrangled from them the last few acres of arable land.

"And your parents?" he asked Luisa, who was fiddling with the plastic-entombed scorpion dangling from his key chain.

"My mother left me to live with my uncle. She works in the city somewhere. I don't remember her name. I don't have a father because he died a long time ago."

The more he listened to her voice, the more he realized that he could not leave her out there. It stung to wonder how long she had been on the street, what countless indecencies she had endured.

"Are you hungry?" he said.

"You can buy me a corn dog," Luisa answered. "And a strawberry Jarritos."

"How are you getting home?" Watching the shop owners close down for the night, he sat down next to her at the edge of a water fountain.

"I will stay in the city and try to make some money. I sleep at the hospital outside the door where they bring in the really sick ones. There are lots of people waiting there, so I'm not afraid. There aren't as many cockroaches, either, and sometimes the people give me food. I once saw this guy who was missing half his face. He was covered in blood and he looked dead. I used to have nightmares about him visiting me at night."

"Do you want to come with me, sleep at my apartment?" he said.

"Do you have a TV?" she asked with the unabashed anticipation that only a child could display.

"No, but I have a radio."

Luisa ate the two *banderillas* and drank the soda he had bought her while they drove to the hotel room Mexicali Rose had allotted him. He knew Rose's spies would be out in full force, so he parked the car two blocks from the hacienda and carried the girl on his shoulders the rest of the way. The Spanish-style ranch house had been graced with the presence of the old-time bandidos and revolutionaries, foreign dignitaries, and insurgent generals. It had subsequently been converted into a Jesuit seminary and finally a military barracks. Abandoned after it had been ravaged by a fire and three floods, Rose had gotten her hands on it, transformed it into its present incarnation: a part-time brothel and full-time headquarters for her international sex trade. He was one of her drivers, shuttling her girls and clients to and from the airport, nightclubs, race track, and other hotels.

Nando was aware of the risk involved in taking the girl to the hotel. It was only a matter of time before Mexicali Rose got word that he was keeping the girl in his room. The alternative, of course, was to leave her out in the street. She had obviously survived out there thus far, but something told him what he had to do. Maybe it was a warped sense of morality or guilt, or some other self-serving emotional hang-up that pricks the human soul into acts of kindness and allows the good inhabitants of the planet to sleep better at night.

"I will please you," Luisa said, touching his chest.

"No," he said, guiding her to the bed. "It's time for sleep."

"Do you think I'm ugly?" Luisa said in a manner that seemed a bit too indignant for a six-year-old.

"I think you're beautiful," he said, handing her the radio headset that managed to strain in an oldies English station from across the border. He usually kept it at his bedside and used it to bat away the unholy visions that encroached on his mind as he waited for sleep to come.

"You must sleep now," he said, but before he had finished the sentence, she had closed her eyes and drifted away into that fast, profound sleep that symbolized all that was simple and good, the kind of sleep he had not experienced for years and probably never would again.

"I hear you have a visitor."

"Just someone I picked up for the night."

"Kind of young, I hear."

"She's old enough."

"She looking for work?"

"Stay away from her."

There was a sound. Footsteps. Familiar. A child. It was Luisa.

Luisa seemed considerably older, despite him not having seen her for two months. She smiled.

"Thought something had happened to you," Luisa said in an accusatory tone. "Who's she?"

"Keep your voice down and don't ask silly questions," said Nando, keeping an eye on the sleeping Xiomara. "Seen any *federales* lately?"

"I saw a regiment in García's café last week. They were asking about Damián Cortez, the *narco*, then they left. Got any candy?"

Nando handed her the last Patito. Her efficient fingers made quick work of the wrapper, and she crammed the treat into her mouth.

"Anybody been snooping around the shed?"

"Just some boys and their girlfriends, drinking and having sex." Luisa was grinning.

"You still liking it here?"

"I want to go with you."

"Not this time."

"When?"

"Soon."

"You promised."

"Yes."

"When are you heading out?"

"Soon as the heat softens a little."

"When are you coming back?"

"I don't know."

He saw the sparkle in Luisa's eyes flicker out.

"Are you going to marry her?"

"She's a client."

"Do you think she is prettier than me?"

"Go now."

"I'm going to come here every day until you come back for me."

Nando watched the girl disappear through a crack in the shed's wall and into the feverish light of the afternoon.

"Who was that?" said Xiomara, rising from her nap.

"A friend," he said, suddenly feeling the tug of sorrow in his belly.

The heat was finally beginning to slacken as the long shadows of early evening crept across the baked dirt. It was time to move out. He would use the hour or so of twilight to advance rapidly through the longest stretch of their journey before nightfall, when everything, including time, would slow to a crawl.

"You ready?" he said.

"Yes," she answered, sighing weightily.

They followed the sandy road out of Villa Oscura and into the desert that seemed especially lonely that evening with its drawn-out murk and ingrained shadows slithering across the vast emptiness. The darkness was playing tricks on his brain. It wasn't that he was tired. Something was different. Perhaps it was the humidity that seemed to thicken the gloom, drowning out the light of the car's headlamps and making his eyes swim in and out of focus. The spell was so potent that he found himself veering off onto the shoulder of the road repeatedly.

At first he was convinced that the glow in the distance was just another optical illusion caused by the night's sorcery. But as his car rounded a brigade of soft hills, he realized that it was, in fact, a magnificent fire burning on the side of the road.

Xiomara sat staring at the fire, her eyes still and brimming with dread. As they drew closer, he could see the charred skeletons of two pickup trucks drowning in the fury of the whipping flames. The gummy, synthetic odor of burned rubber and fiberglass choked the air, but it was mixed with another odor, something distasteful and strangely familiar. And then it came to him as he remembered that hellishly hot afternoon in the desert when he had come upon the pit that spat forth that same candied stink of charred flesh.

"Keep still," he said, as he stopped the car and climbed out.

Nando shielded his face with his hands as the heat blasted his face. Slowly he circled the mass of flames, scanning the darkness for movement. The wind had begun to swirl again, smothering his face with plumes of black smoke, causing his eyes to tear. As he crept closer to the fire, he became aware that all around him the sand glittered with brass 9-mm and .45 shells. A meshwork of tire tracks adorned the sand. He followed them and saw that they became gouged tread marks that trailed off the road and into the night. They had come out of the desert to ambush the pair of trucks now smoldering before him. A gun battle had ensued, then the perpetrators had set the vehicles on fire. As the wind dispersed the intensity of the flames, he edged closer to the vehicles and saw the torched corpses of two men slumped in each cab.

"He's here," Xiomara said, joining him in front of the blaze.

"I don't think so," he said, sweating profusely, yet not entirely because of the fire.

"How do you know?"

"The marking on the sides of the trucks on the bottom of the door."

She strained her eyes and managed to make out the chrome glint of a figurine attached to the bottom of the driver's-side door of each truck, the Aztec god Quetzalcoatl, a symbol Carlos used to brand all of his automobiles. It was his coat of arms, his talisman against *judiciales* and *federales*.

"He wouldn't take out his own men."

"Then who was it?"

"Drug hits aren't this messy."

That instinctive voice of caution in his head suddenly went off again, but there was nowhere to run. They were in the middle of the Área del silencio, the country's most remote and perilous territory, a reputed location for the occurrence of bizarre phenomena that ranged from UFO abductions to ritualistic satanic sacrifices. Serafín had sworn on more than one occasion that on a particular hillside known as Loma macabra, a vehicle left in neutral would roll upward by virtue of some mysterious energy. He didn't know if there was any truth to the stories he had heard throughout the years, yet most of his colleagues did believe them and avoided the area at all costs. The fact was that there was nothing and no one for at least a hundred miles in every direction. If someone was planning a hit, the Área del silencio was where it would go down.

Nando felt the bullet kiss his hipbone long before the sharp retort registered in his eardrums. He bolted for the car, dragging Xiomara behind him. After shoving her in, he dove into the passenger's seat, dodging another bullet, and thrust the car into drive, thankful he had left the engine running. He could hear the onslaught of bullets ripping through the air all around, a series of them peppering the trunk. One of them pulverized the rearview mirror while another slammed into the dashboard, leaving a mess of shattered knobs and twisted plastic. All the while, he kept his head buried beneath the steering wheel, steering with one hand and pinning Xiomara's head downward with the other.

He had yet to establish visual contact with the assailants, who remained shielded by the darkness. There were no headlights, indicating that they were at least as familiar with the roads and terrain as he was. As the shower of bullets stopped momentarily, he raised his head to orient himself. He had run off the road and was speeding along a shallow bank of sand. Gut instinct told him that if he worked the car back onto the road, they would be finished. The only chance was to steer the car as deep into the desert as possible, and that was exactly what he did.

He could feel the wheels of the car cutting deeper and deeper into the sand. It wouldn't be long before they sank into the soft ocean of desert. What then? And the fuel? With as many revolutions as the engine was cranking out, the chase would be a short one, but there was no time to worry about that now. The car suddenly lurched forward and pitched down the precipice of a steep dune. The steering wheel flew from his hand as the tires were jarred to one side and locked in place by the pressure of the sand. Xiomara was screaming as the car began a series of slow rolls down to the bottom of the dune. He tried desperately to pull her toward him, hoping to cushion her from the impact that would come any moment.

Seconds later, he lay on his back in the sand-choked darkness, wondering if he was still alive or if the pitch black that engulfed his senses were some preliminary stage of death. A racing heartbeat and a throbbing ache in his shoulder verified that he was still among the living. He heard a muffled groan close by.

"Are you hurt?" Nando said.

"Nothing serious," Xiomara answered.

"Try not to move. They're watching us."

They both stopped breathing when they heard the grinding engines overhead and saw the floodlights scanning the bottom of the dune into which they had tumbled. Two distinguishable voices came down faintly yet clear.

"Go check it."

"Fuck that. I'll be trapped down there."

"Would you prefer a bullet in the head?"

"Relax. It's at least a hundred feet down. No way they survived, and even if they did, it won't be for long. They'll roast out here tomorrow if the coyotes don't eat them before then."

"If they do survive, you'll wish you were dead. Check it."

Someone cocked a gun.

"*Culero.*"

The hiss of sand cascading down the side of the dune slithered through the darkness.

"They're coming," Xiomara insisted.

He looked around him and realized that the hood of the car had been crushed down the middle, pinning him between the dashboard and the windshield, effectively cutting him off from the girl and any viable exit.

"Get out," he shouted, figuring that she would have a good head start if he kept them occupied.

The rustle of the sand was getting louder. They were mere paces away. Even the clatter of their firearms could now be heard. They would descend upon the car and spray it with bullets or set it on fire, something inarguably torturous and annihilative like that. He listened as Xiomara squirmed through the tattered upholstery, broken glass, and twisted metal of the car's interior.

"I'm here," she said, peering at him through the windshield.

"Go," he said, hearing the string of footsteps. She was gone seconds before the footsteps reached the wreckage. He took a deep breath and held it, lowering his eyelids, but allowing a tiny slit through which he could orient himself, a trick he had perfected during childhood when he pretended to be asleep to avoid his drunk father's rage.

Amazingly, he was able to see the stalker coming. He felt a twinge of relief when he saw only one pair of legs skirting the car, but that quickly dissipated when the nose of the AK-47 appeared right behind them. The man squatted, craning his head downward and into the car to inspect its contents, the barrel of the automatic rifle tucked almost under his chin.

"I see the smuggler," he called.

"What about the other one?" came the voice from above.

"I can't tell. The car's pretty fucked up. She's probably somewhere underneath."

"Secure him, then search the area. If she got out, she couldn't have gotten far."

A sharp, quick explosion that seemed to have origi-

nated from somewhere behind him shattered the darkness. Before the man's face hit the sand, a full-throttle stac-
cato of AK-47 slugs ripped through the body of the car. A
white-hot strobe of pain seared across his thigh as one of
the bullets bore through the flesh above his right knee.
Another quick string of rounds shredded the darkness as
he applied pressure to his thigh, already warm and greasy
with blood.

There was only silence and dusty light.

"Don't move."

The voice startled him and touched off a fresh wave of
pain up his leg and across his stomach and chest as his
body instinctively cringed.

It was Xiomara.

"I'm hit," he said.

"Don't move," she reiterated. "I'm going to get you out."

Three shots rang out, followed by the rough sprin-
kling of splintered glass as the girl pounded the shattered
windshield with a barrage of kicks. Nando covered his
head as she broke through the windshield and cleared
away the glass.

"Give me your hand," she said.

He looked back above his shoulder and saw the slim
silhouette extending a small hand toward his face. The
other hand held a gun. It was torture trying to extend his
own hand, stretching his body and aggravating the bullet
wound, which now throbbed with nauseating force. But
he knew there was no other way. Even with the windshield busted out, he could generate neither the leverage
nor the strength to worm through. Alone, Xiomara was
probably not strong enough to pull him out. It would
require a combination of both their efforts to liberate him,
and so he reached out as far as he could while currents of
pain jolted his body.

The sensation of her deft fingertips probing across his
arms ignited a flush of reassurance in the front of his

brain. She reached into the gaping windshield frame and clasped his wrist with both of her hands, pulling with all her weight. Her strength was astonishing. Slowly he felt his legs begin to dislodge from within the car's mangled entrails, and his body spilled out onto the cold sand. It was only after he lay on the desert floor and the adrenaline began to subside that he realized that his thigh had caught on the glass-rimmed edges of the windshield frame, gouging the flesh above the bullet wound.

"What happened?" he mumbled.

"Those were not trained killers. They were probably a couple of hired rural thugs who can barely write their names, let alone properly aim a gun. I just watched for the flares of their guns each time they shot."

"How?"

"Are you some kind of secret government agent?"

"How bad is it?"

"You've lost a lot of blood, don't move."

She was gone even before the sound of her voice had faded.

What remained of his strength was waning rapidly. He felt a curious urge to laugh out loud, probably would have if his physical condition had permitted it. Some kind of bad ass, he heard his father's voice echo in the back of his mind, the sarcasm so heavy he could taste it like the acrid juice of lemon. But there was something else surging through the short-circuiting network of perception, something warm and fleeting that allowed him to close his eyes and rest until the grind of her feet upon the sand brought him back.

"It's going to hurt," she said, kneeling beside him and gently sliding her outstretched palms underneath his calves. He clamped his eyes and winced as she lifted his leg slightly upward. He shuddered and held his breath as he fought the cloud bank of unconsciousness that was sweeping across his brain. He saw a wedge light and a spark, then nothing.

The chill of early night was gnawing at his bones when he regained consciousness. There was no pain until he tried to move. A thin moan squirted through his throat as he opened his eyes to a glorious bank of stars. Orion's belt was high and prominent just above his head. The backs of his eyes ached, and his lips felt like they had been sealed with Super Glue. Despite the pain, he allowed himself to shiver. It was comforting perhaps only because it confirmed that he was still alive and cognizant enough to feel discomfort.

"I thought you were going to die," said the voice.

"Where am I?" he said, turning his head and seeing the thick, heavily treaded tires of an off-road vehicle inches from his face. Again, he tried to move, managing to roll over onto his side and provoking a fresh assault of pain. A pair of hands hooked his arms and lifted him to a sitting position against one of the enormous tires.

"Here," said the voice. A bottle of Presidente brandy appeared in front of his face. He plucked the bottle from the air and unscrewed its red plastic cap.

"Found it in the truck," the voice said.

"What happened?" he said, grimacing at the sweet burn of the brandy as it scorched his tongue and throat.

"We were ambushed. They chased us into the desert, and we wound up down there." He looked at the drop that opened up a few feet from the front of the vehicle. Pieces of the night's chaos flashed in his head. The bright headlights, the chase, the crash, and the ensuing gunfight. His brain throbbed, and he took another drag from the bottle.

"You were trapped in the car. I got you out and pulled you up with a rope I found in the trunk of the car. You were unconscious the whole time."

"You killed them?"

"They are dead."

"The car?"

"Destroyed, but the truck works, and it's got a little more than half a tank."

"We can make it."

"Maybe, but that's not the real problem. They were ahead of us."

That was when he saw his wound, or what had become of it. It was wrapped in a tangle of elastic lace and silk. Even in the weak light of the truck's headlights, it didn't take him long to recognize the components of the makeshift bandage. He reached down and touched the soft fabric. It was wet.

"Alcohol," she said. "I apologize if it embarrasses you, but there was nothing else. You would have bled to death."

He tried to smile but failed. "Thank you," he said, taking several deep swigs of brandy. It numbed his tongue and loosened his jaw. His mind yearned for that murky, thought-deluding pool of intoxication.

"You need a doctor," she said, tossing the items she had rescued from the wreckage into the back of the truck. Her movements were taut, purposeful, yet unmistakably feminine. "It will eventually become infected."

"You'll have to drive."

"I've never driven a car."

"Does it have a gearshift on the left side of the driver's seat, or is it up next to the steering wheel?"

"It's by the steering wheel."

"It's an automatic. No sweat."

He recapped the liquor bottle and dropped it onto the sand, afraid one more drink would send him to the place his father had called the time machine, that state of drunken bliss from which one emerged days later with a lifetime worth of regret and one bitch of a hangover. Although he wasn't a stranger to either, there were, in fact, more pressing issues at hand. Staying alive, for starters.

The girl promptly fished the bottle from the sand. "We may need this later," she said.

"Yes," he said, wondering if his brain had not already engaged the time machine.

Riding her firm, bony shoulder, Nando climbed into the dingy confines of the Ford Bronco. It smelled of cigarette smoke, old vinyl, and alcohol that had been evaporated through the pores of those who had drunk it. From the rearview mirror dangled a small silver-encased portrait of the Virgen de Guadalupe on a braided leather strap.

His head began to sway as the truck crept across the desert floor. Xiomara clung to the steering wheel, staring hypnotically forward, her body stiffly perched on the dusty seat. Nando smiled at the thought of his savior possessing the driving skills of an adolescent with a week-old driver's license.

"Just remember to press the big pedal on the left side with your foot while you move the gear shift from P to D," Nando instructed. "Then slowly let go of the pedal. When the car starts to move, slowly tap the pedal on the right to speed up. Follow the tire tracks to the road."

He closed his eyes hoping that this could quell the buoyant nausea, a symptom of the motion sickness he experienced whenever he rode shotgun, or in the backseat of anything with four tires, that was swirling in his stomach. The truck's bad suspension and the undulating roll of the sand only made it worse.

"Turn the lights off."

"I can't see."

"It will get easier as dawn draws near."

"I don't know if I can do it."

"Concentrate on the truck's movement, on the fluidity of the tires, any change in the way they respond to the ground. You'll know if you start to stray."

"I wish I had some music."

He marveled at the way in which Xiomara was at once unyielding and vulnerable. Even in his state, he could sense the defiance that swam off her like currents of electricity, pulsing from her eyes, her hair, her shoulders and hips. Her beauty was like a stone-sharpened knife, the kind of brutal perfection you cannot examine for a prolonged period of time because everything else, even one's own life, seems irrelevant.

Nando leaned back into the dusty seat and watched as the looming dawn painted the desert the color of fast dreams. The image besieged his chest with a rushed heaviness, a hollow anticipation that always seemed the prelude of a revelation.

"You know," he said, his brain swimming in charged vapors of the brandy, "when I was a kid, I used to love getting up in the morning before sunrise. I used to think how everything was so perfect in that pale light, the whole world innocent and good. When I grew old enough to know better, I consoled myself with the realization that it was always morning somewhere on the planet, that the newness being played out before me was being experienced by someone every second of every day."

"If you could do anything, go anywhere, what would it be?"

"Somewhere on the beach, away from tourists and noise and smog. Just me, maybe my brother, with nothing but the sunset to tell us that time was passing."

"You'll get to do that," she said.

"I'm not counting on it. I've learned not to expect anything. It's just that much harder to accept when something you've been waiting for doesn't happen. You?"

"I always wanted to travel to someplace across the ocean, to China or Australia or someplace like that. I'd set out on a boat and let the wind decide."

He could feel the telepathic ripple of a smile. He suddenly found his mind wading in memories that had abandoned his brain for years, the grind of the propane delivery truck outside his bedroom window, the icy bite of the concrete floor upon his feet, his mother humming some impromptu melody as she prepared a breakfast of boiled milk and oatmeal for him and his brothers and sisters. There were the houses, cold, broken, infested with roaches, all of them a favor from an acquaintance or an act of mercy from a resourceful member of the parish, charity for a family whose drunk father was laying in some shit-covered alleyway of the town, his face simmering in a two-day-old soup of vomit and dead flies.

It was hot that day. He remembered the sun stinging the back of his neck as he walked home from school. He made it a rule to avoid the main thoroughfare, the shortest route to the house, but he didn't want to risk seeing his father sitting on the sidewalk in front of the cantina, conscious only because he had run out of money. He would look up when Nando walked by and plead for a couple of pesos, just enough for the two shots of tequila that would short-circuit his brain, his eyes desperate and filled with agony, yet failing to recognize his own son.

Nando had reconsidered that day, having been kept late at school by his algebra teacher who wanted to review a homework assignment. He had promised to escort his mother on a delivery to Divina Luz, the sector of town where the only thing more dangerous than walking the streets with several hundred pesos' worth of consumer goods was brandishing a municipal police badge in front of the loitering bands of cement-sniffing barrio zombies that populated the streets at night. She had urged him to arrive early so that they could be out of there by dark.

He was stopped by Don Luis as he passed the cantina. "*Hijo*," he said, "your father is bad off." He pointed toward the dirt lot behind the cantina. "Go. See if you can take him home."

Nando found him lying face down, motionless, his

pants smeared and stinking. There was blood on the ground, dried and blackened by the sun. He gently lifted his father's head and saw the shattered stump of his nose. He had fallen face first, probably knocking himself out cold. His eyes were open, and for a moment Nando thought that his father was dead. A black, phlegmy liquid began oozing from a corner of his mouth as low gurgling sounds surfaced from his throat. He sprinted home and found his mother waiting for him, her shoulder bag and shawl ready.

"What's wrong?" she asked when she saw that he had been crying.

Although he wanted desperately to tell her what he had seen, he couldn't because he knew how much she still loved the man, despite the drinking and the beatings and the destitution he had inflicted upon them. It would have broken her completely. Two days later his father showed up while they were having dinner. He ate, showered, and forced his mother into the bedroom before disappearing into the night again.

A sharp exclamation that was more breath than sound shook him awake. Xiomara bore a panicked expression as she gripped the steering wheel.

"What's wrong?" he said.

"Nothing. I thought I had lost the tracks."

"You're doing fine. Haven't slipped once."

"I think this voodoo driving system you've developed is bullshit and that you're just trying to convince me we're not going to die. How's your thigh?"

"Finely dressed."

He tried to sound as convincing as possible. Yet he knew that if he wanted to keep his leg, he needed medical attention within two, three hours, at most. "The brandy numbed it a bit, feels a lot better."

He cringed at the desperation of the lie. The brandy had numbed nothing more than his brain. And although it had taken the edge off the pain, he felt his strength evaporating into the cool dawn air as intermittent spells of fever and chills began wracking his body.

"You have a complete soul," she said.

For a moment he thought he had dozed off and that the voice he had heard was a byproduct of his anesthetized subconscious.

"My mother used to say that the greatest mistake we can make as humans is to ignore the beauty of the world around us because it was meant for us to witness, to give us hope, because only then would our souls be complete. What you said about the dawn made me think of that."

"What?"

"Childhood. The thing I remember most is that I hated to leave Ave Blanca because when I returned, everything had changed. The people, the streets, and the lay of the land remained the same, but somehow the essence of my world had shifted like a sagging portrait on a wall. I felt disoriented, almost as if the place I had visited had superimposed itself on the familiar one, or that part of me had been left behind. It haunted me for days."

"This one will be hard to overcome," he said.

"Rest," she said.

His thoughts trailed back to the day before in the shed when he had tried to prey on her. He wanted to weep from the shame. He had to get her out of that desert. Even if he didn't make it, he had to get her to Tokyo.

"Follow the road until it ends," he said. "You'll see a dump." He was finding it increasingly difficult to mold the words.

"Then what?

"Tokyo."

Then the words disintegrated completely. All he could

do was wait and hope that the woman who had saved his life had enough sense to save her own. He could feel them not far behind. He would probably be dead when Rivas caught up to them, but she would still be alive.

Xiomara drove slow but hard, edging the wheels of the truck cautiously over the cracked, eroded swath of ground that at times became so slack that it seemed to have brought the truck to a halt. She had never felt more vulnerable in her life. All around her time had frozen. Even the presence of the smuggler, who had slumped down into the seat with his head against the window, did nothing to stem the sensation that there was no living thing except her for miles. She almost laughed when she looked at the bandage she had fastened to his leg. She had been wearing that underwear for days.

The soothing glow of dawn loomed just beyond the pitched eastern horizon that throbbed like a groggy eyelid. It felt like the ground was dissolving beneath her as she stared north along the meandering road that was really nothing more than a slightly worn footpath barely distinguishable from the terrain on each side of it. She thought of the finality of certain moments in life when it seemed that nothing else existed outside the realm of her own consciousness. It was hard to consider that there might be something good anywhere in the world at that moment. Xiomara suddenly understood what the smuggler had said about his love of the dawn during his childhood. It made it difficult to concentrate on matters at hand. Unfortunate, to say the least, because time was running out. She could taste death in each breath she drew. Its residue was all around her, on her clothes, in her hair, and on her skin; a dry, hollow scent that made her want to scream.

El Apocalipsis

As they neared the city, the road veered eastward through the sand dunes and saguaro cacti that encircled the low-lying stretch of desert canyon into which Ciudad Juárez, and a good portion of El Paso as well, had been embedded. Xiomara began to make out the glint of the glass on some of the skyscrapers as the sunlight bled over the horizon. She could see the gray specter of the unzoned shantytowns and tenements that had sprung up on the hillsides around the city.

In the North, living in the hills was a mark of affluence and privilege. It represented an exotic lifestyle that only the prosperous and fortunate, such as doctors, lawyers, movie stars, and politicians, could enjoy and aspire to achieve. It was a life of exotic architecture, swimming pools, gated estates, and domestic servants. In her county, living in the hills was a sign of struggle. No one cared about the hills, it was a no man's land, too expensive to develop or maintain. Its inhabitants, mostly migrants and the displaced, or those displaced from more desirable living conditions in the city, were allowed to settle there at will. The official municipality claimed no jurisdiction and no responsibility to these hillside communities. Homes went without running water or electricity. There were no garbage collectors, no neighborhood associations, no maintenance crews, no police, firemen, or ambulances.

It was a tenuous existence at best. Adapting to their austere reality, those who chose to live on the hills always learned to appreciate and even enjoy the fact that they had a place to sleep, eat, and raise children. They shared a sense of accomplishment that they had, regardless of the countless luxuries they could not experience, slain the beast of destitution, for they had succeeded in avoiding the streets and alleyways, the riverbanks or the city dump, places of horror and holocaust that promised only misery, places that fell between reality and a nightmare where good fortune could be claimed by making it through the day alive or without having watched a loved one starve or freeze to death or get raped, places like the Ciudad Juárez landfill, last stop for the Nando Flores Express.

The smoke signaled their arrival, that and the rancid stench of decay that began to penetrate the Bronco. The car smuggler was bathed in sweat, and Xiomara considered that was a good indication that he was still alive. She wasn't sure what kind of medical attention, if any, would be available where they were headed. If the man died, it would be one more on her conscience. Even now with a hit squad pursuing her, it had been the smuggler who had suffered her fate, Marina before him, and Germán and both her parents.

Xiomara hoped he—God, she couldn't even remember his name, Nando something—would live long enough to enjoy the money that was coming to him. Maybe he would take it and get as far away from the border as he could. She sure as hell planned to.

The sandy contour of the road eventually gave way to a gray, sour-smelling ooze that clung to the tires of the Bronco, causing them to spin often without gripping the road. The landfill began as a series of greenish wastewater treatment ponds aligned in three rows of four at the foot of a large butte that rose like the petrified corpse of some desert nomad at the city's eastern edge. The foulness of the fumes emanating from the toxic water would have been unbearable had it not been for a sweet morning breeze that blew off the butte and diluted the pestilence. Beyond the cesspools lay a cemetery of broken city bus shells, an old backhoe and road grader that looked like the skeletons of large, prehistoric beasts, and two military warplanes that had been clipped of their wings.

Then the garbage piles came into view: acres and acres of the city's refuse and waste. Thick, black smoke billowed from a sector of the landfill where the garbage was apparently being incinerated. A large flock of gulls hovered above the smoke, undaunted by the soot. A few yards beyond the garbage heaps Xiomara could make out a panorama of roofless huts, cardboard lean-tos, and triangular shacks that were indistinguishable from the rest of the landfill, except that there were people huddled around cooking fires outside the makeshift dwellings.

"We're here," she announced, hoping the car smuggler would respond. He issued a shallow groan but nothing more. She would have to find the man named Tokyo herself. They were now in the middle of the dump, surrounded by dirty, unrecognizable birds that trembled in their sleep as the pickup slid by, and that ever-thickening stench that clung to everything. It seemed that the whole world was rotting. It was the smell of absolute decay, of the dead and the dying, of discarded and forgotten life, the loss of hope.

As the Bronco rounded one of the garbage heaps, she saw a small barefoot girl prodding the carcass of a horse with a stick.

"I'm looking for a man called Tokyo," she yelled to the girl, who donned a puzzled look.

"Do you have any food?" said the girl.

"No, but I can help you find some."

The little girl flung the stick at the dead horse and jumped onto the step-board on the passenger side of the Bronco. "Over there," she said, pointing to a pair of wooden shelters whose inhabitants had already noticed the strange automobile that had come out of the desert and into their world.

"You have no business on that truck," growled a man who was standing in front of one of the wooden shelters. "Get down."

"She is going to give me food," squealed the girl as she jumped off the Bronco.

"You're crazy," said the man. He was tall and dangerously thin. A sparse beard crawled along his jawbone and cheeks. His clothes were torn and muddy, and he wore a mismatched Nike running shoe with an old, unlaced work boot. As he drew closer, Xiomara could see that he was missing several teeth and that his arms and neck were covered with jagged, red sores.

"Who are you?" the man insisted.

"I'm sorry to intrude," she answered. "I am looking for one of your neighbors. A man they call Tokyo."

"He is not my neighbor. Lives farther up the road near the recycling center."

"Can you take me to him?"

"If you were wise, you'd stay clear of that man. He is possessed by a demon."

"I need to speak to him. Your daughter said she knew where he lived. My friend is in need of his assistance. I will pay you to take me to him."

By now a large woman in a long dress and a shawl emerged from the dwelling, one of her legs bore the same lesions that marked the man's skin.

"She is not my daughter," said the man, swiping a large fly from a corner of his mouth. "She crawled out of the dump a few months ago. My sister and I took her in."

"Please. My friend will die if I do not take him to see this man."

"Pay me first," said the man, "and I will take you."

She handed him a one-hundred-peso bill and the half-full bottle of Presidente. The man's eyes brightened. He seemed almost healthy at the sight of the bill, which he quickly held up for his sister and the little girl to admire like some rare artifact that he had dug out of the muck. Immediately, he emptied the half bottle of brandy into his quivering throat and gave the empty bottle to his sister.

"Do you have some chocolate milk?" asked the little girl, smiling.

The man walked alongside the Bronco as she edged it along a rivulet of black sludge. Several other dump dwellers were up and about now, foraging through the garbage piles, erecting new shelters, and tending steaming pots that hung above cooking fires. Her confused stomach ached with anticipation as she caught the familiar whiffs of baking tortillas and coffee, yet convulsed at the sight of the piles of human waste that were scattered all over the ground.

Xiomara could see that even in the dump, there was a class distinction among the inhabitants. Some of them had managed to construct impressive shelters complete with windows, garages, and small pens for chickens and swine. She even saw one of the dwellings sporting a mini satellite dish on its aluminum roof.

"He lives there," said the man, pointing to a garage attached to a hovel that had been gutted by fire. Without waiting for a response, he set off at a frantic pace back down the muddy trail toward his shanty.

The misshapen hut sported large strips of fungus and moss that crawled up its sides like tentacles. Large piles of earth had accumulated at the back and side walls as if someone had tried to bury the entire thing but failed. Before she could open the car door, a raging Doberman pinscher leaped into her face. She quickly rolled up the window, hoping the glass would hold off the ramming snout of the dog that quickly coated the entire window with a thick froth.

The day disappeared as quickly as it had materialized.

When she looked through the window again, she saw a small man, neatly dressed in a black jogging suit and high-top basketball shoes, balancing a pistol on his bony outstretched arm and the dog at his heels.

"You ever see a dog eat a person? They go for the face first. I wouldn't even have to waste a bullet. Even if they heard you screaming, nobody would give a shit."

He was less than small; he was a miniature man. His mustache was perfectly clipped into a sleek arc no bigger than an eyebrow, and his hair, slick and curly with grease, was styled in a classic mullet so as to accentuate a pair of diamond earrings and a tangled sheen of gold chains around his neck that matched the outlines of his two front teeth. Yet it was his eyes that most astonished her: a pair of small, slit-like indentations that gave him a slight Asian hint and looked not at her but beyond her.

"Are you the man they call Tokyo?"

The man's jaw suddenly clenched, his eyes rolling back into his head. "No one uses that name around here unless they have been given permission to do so," he said after recovering. "Who sent you?"

She pointed to the car smuggler, who had managed to uncap an eye that was keenly fixed on the spasmodic midget.

"What's wrong with him?" said Tokyo, the sharpness in his voice ebbing.

"He's been shot in the leg," she said. "I stopped the bleeding, but it's probably already infected."

"Bring him in."

The interior of the garage was tidy, amply furnished, and somewhat insulated from the landfill's stink, even though it could not have been more than twenty yards away from the foulest section of the landfill. The sign next to the garage warned trespassers that it was where hospital and industrial toxic wastes were dumped. Her feet had crunched over several hypodermic needles, plastic tubes, and latex gloves as she had helped carry the car smuggler into the garage.

In one corner of the room was a large, flat-screen television stocked with dozens of pornographic videocassettes—contraband by the looks of grisly scenes depicted on the dust jackets— and a workstation with a laptop computer, a police scanner, and several cell phones in the other corner. The kitchen consisted of a water spigot that snaked in from the outside, a rusty TV dinner tray, and stacks of canned soup and prepackaged noodles. An intricate-looking bookshelf stereo hung on the wall above a fish tank with a school of multicolored goldfish, opposite a freestanding punching bag and a rack of shiny jogging suits, all of them either black or gray. A red recliner stood in the middle of the garage like a sentry. The only thing she did not see was a bathroom, which was understandable since already they were having trouble negotiating the cramped space with Nando stretched out on the floor on top of a futon mattress.

Tokyo lifted Nando's arms and legs as Xiomara undressed him and then cleaned the smuggler's entire body with a damp cloth, applying rubbing alcohol to his chest and neck. While the little man measured several powdery substances from clear, plastic bags, mixing them with tequila in a small pot, she fed him doses of a brownish liquid Tokyo had dispensed from an aluminum thermos with the end of a straw, capping the other end with her thumb to create a vacuum and prevent the liquid from spilling.

"Nice bandage," said Tokyo as he uncovered the wound dressing she had fashioned. Using a thin paintbrush, he began to apply the gummy mixture he had prepared onto Nando's wound. The car smuggler began to moan and toss his body from one side to the other.

"It would be worse if you had not given him the potion," said Tokyo.

"What is it?" she inquired.

"Mint tea laced with peyote."

"What about the stuff you're putting on his leg?"

"A mixture of agave, ocotillo, and creosote bush. It will clean the infection. It's also good for sunburn and arthritis."

After Tokyo had finished dressing the wound with a fresh bandage, they covered Nando with an old San Marcos blanket imprinted with a pair of maroon deer drinking out of a woodland pool. She retrieved the damp cloth and continued to run it over his forehead, cheeks, and mouth. His bronze-colored body looked like it had been run through a meat grinder. There was an old knife wound on his right forearm and another just below his right breast. A squid-shaped burn mark covered his entire left bicep. His abdomen harbored the centipede memoir of an appendectomy, and his thighs were a battlefield of welts, scabs, and bruises. It was the tattoo that intrigued her the most: A young, pretty woman with fair hair and thin, looping letters that spelled out *Por ti todo, Mya*. She ran her fingers over the grayish ink.

"So what kind of trouble is Nando in this time?" said Tokyo, prying open one of the soup cans with the tip of a butcher knife.

"I hired him to bring me here. We were ambushed by bandits."

"First time I ever heard of someone hiring a coyote before they got to the border, unless, of course, you're from Central America."

"I didn't say I wanted to cross. I just needed a guide to bring me to Juárez."

"Would have been safer and cheaper if you had taken the bus."

"I was desperate."

"I don't think you know the meaning of the word *desperation*. Ever know a mother who has to feed her starving children the rotting flank of a dog because there is nothing else, or a man whose brain is so traumatized by the horrors he has seen that he rolls around in his own shit? The dump is filled with young women who have to walk four miles to work in a place where they are degraded and harassed, not knowing if they'll make it home alive, just to make enough money to buy a stack of tortillas. Ever known that kind of desperation?"

"Look, might it have occurred to you that whatever business I have here doesn't concern you?"

"You're in my home. Therefore, I must consider that whatever happened to the car smuggler can happen to me. So until you leave, your business does concern me."

Suddenly, the soup can he had been holding slipped from his hands, its contents splattering on the floor. The man had become a convulsing knot of clenched muscle, his entire body contorted in a demonstration of pain. His fingers were hooked like claws, and his feet were tucked tightly against his stomach like the haunches of a dog. His gaping mouth was frozen in a silent scream, leaking globules of white, foamy saliva, while his eyes rolled and fluttered behind half-closed lids.

Xiomara recoiled, initially suspicious of a crude though well-orchestrated joke intended to frighten her into revealing the true nature of her circumstances. But when the twisted, gyrating shape began to slam itself against the floor and utter a noise that sounded like a hungry calf, she knew it was no act. She saw the butcher knife he had used to open the soup can and thought about lunging for it before his body fell on top of it, but just as suddenly his convulsions ceased.

"I beg your pardon," said a flustered and embarrassed Tokyo. "Sometimes I get them three and four times a day. Other times I go for weeks without one. The people around here think I'm possessed by the devil. They even sent one of the missionaries from the north to cure me."

"I didn't mean to be discourteous."

"My contacts tell me there is an unusual level of activity on the network, hits going down, contracts being issued. There's one out there for a young woman posing as a migrant. One million dollars. You know anything about that?"

"I should have figured you were only too willing to help us. Is he in on it, too?"

"Relax. I'm a goods dealer, not a mercenary, although I'd be lying if I told you it hadn't crossed my mind. I'll tell you one thing, your friend here chose a good hiding spot. They won't come in here, nobody will. They're waiting for you to surface somewhere in the city. Then you're theirs. I hope you have a plan."

She felt stupid, then, overwhelmed by the concept of her reality. Yes, she had a plan, a plan contingent on the one variable that was impossible to gauge: the trustworthiness of a man whom she had never met. If this dump dweller—however well connected he was—already knew of what she was attempting, how was she going to get across the border, let alone broker a deal with drug agents for her freedom?

"Ever heard of a reporter named Spanich?" she said.

"El Felino. Of course, I've heard of him. He's mythical in this city."

"El Felino?"

"They call him that because of the countless times he's escaped death. He's got connections to both the Arquimedes-Savón and Baja-Cruz camps. He claims he's merely exercising his privileges as a journalist. Some say he's a double agent on the payroll of both cartels, others claim he's an *ojo*, a spy for the North. They have threatened to shut down the border if any of the contracts on him are carried out."

"I heard he helps people."

"If you've got dealings with El Felino, you must be

into some heavy shit. You've got to be careful, though. There isn't such a thing as privileged information in this city. Everybody knows everybody else's business."

The car smuggler was talking in his sleep. It was tongue-clogged gibberish that made him sound like a helpless infant. Yet there was something endearing about it, something that made her want to lean in close to his ear and whisper that everything was all right.

"You hungry?" said Tokyo, opening a fresh can of soup. "Doesn't taste bad cold after you get past the way it looks. It's not a good idea to build a fire in this part of the dump. Couple of days ago a man blew himself up after igniting some of the methane fumes when he dropped a cigarette butt into one of the garbage heaps. You probably saw the smoke when you came into the landfill. There are actually little pockets in the garbage where the fumes escape from the decomposing material below. Some of the dwellers have tried to build a pipeline from the garbage to their houses for heating during the winter, but it's too dangerous. The fumes aren't as concentrated here, but I'm not willing to take a chance."

"No, thank you," she said.

"You should get some sleep. Not much else to do around here except sift through the garbage. You're safe. Calvo's out there patrolling the yard."

She didn't even have time to worry. The minute she dropped her eyelids, she was out, right there on the hard, clammy floor, with the smell of excrement and blood and death all around.

Xiomara had used her arm as a pillow to sleep on. When she awoke, the circulation had been cut off from her arm for so long that she lost all sensation in it except that unnerving tingle that felt like a million ants under her skin. It was only after she sat up that the feeling began to return to her fingers. She scanned the room for Tokyo, but he was gone.

"I killed them."

The voice startled her, and she gasped as she sprang to her knees, ready to do battle with the disembodied voice. Nando was sitting upright as well, massaging the upper portion of his thigh, his face solemn, his gaze distant.

"What time is it?"

"I could have saved them, but chose not to," he said, ignoring her question.

She could see the grief on his face like a death mask and understood the prudence of silence.

"I wanted to stop them. The heat was killing everybody, even the ones who had no business out in the desert. All I had to do was back off. The coyote insisted that they could resist that heat, that they were used to it, that there would be water in the ravines and places to take shade. But you know what made me go through with it and pile them into that truck and drive them out to the middle of hell? It was the thought that I couldn't deprive them of their right to seek whatever it was they hoped to find at the end of that desert. They died trying to drink each other's piss."

"Sometimes we unwittingly get hooked into doing things that end badly and . . ."

"I'm sick of death. I'm sick of this place, the stench, the noise, the heat, sick of being so irrelevant."

"The question is, do you have the courage to change your life?"

"I wish I did."

She crawled to his side and placed a hand on his forehead. "Fever's gone." she said. "It looks like you'll live."

"I dreamed that I had died."

"You almost did."

"It wasn't a bad feeling. It was like swimming in a warm ocean, letting the current carry me farther and farther away into the horizon. Only it wasn't really an ocean, but a pair of giant hands cupped together to hold the water. At some point I figured that the hands belonged to you."

"It was the peyote that Tokyo gave you."

"I have to give it to you . . ."

"What?"

"For finding Tokyo. Most smugglers on their best days can't find him in all this garbage, and it's not like he appreciates being found."

"Seems to be fond of you, though."

"We go back."

There was a warmth she had not felt before coursing through her body as she sat next to him. It was like a memory or a pleasant thought. It allowed her to breathe and consider the idea that she had made it to Juárez, that she was literally only miles from freedom and a new life. She felt an urge to tell him something that would make him forget his pain, that she was glad he was alive.

"Are you hungry?" she said.

"Just thirsty."

After rummaging through the dark garage, she found an old aluminum canteen insulated in leather. The water smelled stale but it was that or nothing. She returned to Nando and lowered the spout of the canteen to his lips, then took a swallow herself. It tasted good and sweet.

"I wonder where he could be."

"Had to get rid of the truck, look around, see what the climate is, basically trying to figure out how much of a liability we are."

"And here I thought you were friends."

"There's a saying among our creed: a friendship is stable as long as business is good."

She tried to help him dress, but he refused, bidding her to turn her back as he undertook the excruciating task of slipping on his pants. When he had finished, she walked him to the recliner, where he collapsed in exhaustion. Securing his wounded leg onto the footrest, she brought him the water again.

"Looks like I'll be owing you," he said.

"I got you into this. It's the least I can do."

"I figure in the next day or so, I'll be able to move around by myself. Then we can go talk to Spanich."

"Tokyo says they already know about us. Well, about me."

"You were right the first time. There's no going back. They're not going to stop until we're both dead or until they think we're dead. At least you have an idea of where you're headed. It will be more difficult for them to track you down in the North. If you've got the U.S. government helping you, it will be that much better. I hear they change people's identities and put them in safe places. You could ask them to do that for you."

"Ever thought about going north yourself?"

"Yes, but I figure if I'm going to die, it might as well be in my own country. Without money or an education, the North is just a change of address, not much better than here, quite often worse."

"You sound like someone I used to know."

Both of them shrank as Calvo's barking cracked the darkness. They could hear approaching footsteps on the mud outside. Nando removed his belt and wrapped it around his hand, leaving the buckle free. Seconds later, Tokyo's diminutive shape floated through the doorway.

"There's a whole army out there looking for you," he said, locking the door behind him.

"Don't worry," said Nando, "we'll be out of here by morning."

"Doesn't matter. Either way, I'm getting the fuck out. Villa Oscura sounds good right about now. If they catch you, it won't take long for them to follow the trail here."

"I owe you big," said Nando.

"Just don't get killed," said Tokyo, looking at both of them. "I got rid of the truck. Your car is waiting for you at the garage. I got this for you. Figured you would be starving by now. I also brought you some painkillers. I know the peyote is nice, but I wouldn't want cobwebs in my brain if I were in your shoes."

He handed Xiomara the paper bag that he had been carrying. She opened it and removed two sandwiches, two orange-flavored sodas, and a small, white plastic bottle. The two of them ate quietly while their host worked his cell phone, emptied a bottle of *mescal*, and fought off the demons.

The morning brought with it a torrential storm of rain and gusting winds that threatened to splinter the tiny garage. Nando had managed to change the dressing on his wound and confirmed that he was in fact on his way toward recovery by wringing out a few paces with his bad leg. Still, the pain was immense despite the black-market morphine Tokyo had prescribed. Tokyo spent most of the morning tidying up, taking out the trash, and washing the few dishes that had been scattered throughout the garage. He retrieved a bucket of fresh rainwater from the roof of the garage and offered it to Xiomara. Grateful, she proceeded to wash her face, her neck, arms, legs, and feet with a lather of water and dishwashing soap.

"Days like these make you think that the end of the world is here," said Tokyo as he fought back a river of sludge that had crept into the garage through the bottom of the door.

"Every time we had a storm like this back home, the old women of the town swore that *el apocalipsis* was at hand." Xiomara recalled. "Some of them would barricade themselves in their homes to pray. One time, they got this crazy idea that they would all go to the church and await the rapture. They prayed for deliverance, and it came. A mudslide buried the church and everyone in it. My mother said it was punishment from God for their arrogance, thinking that the end of the world was so trivial that a few illiterate crones could predict it."

"End of the world happens every day," said Nando. Turning to Xiomara, Nando said, "I think it's time to make the call."

"Where are you?" said the frantic voice on the other end of the line.

"Close," she said.

"I was worried you had been captured. My informants say there's something big going down. They say the *permiso* is going to be awarded soon, and there's talk that the North is going to nix certification, so the government is trying to find a way to prove their commitment to the cause. I also heard Baja-Cruz has matched the Arquimedes-Savón bounty. The latest word is that Arquimedes-Savón will let the person who brings you in name his price."

"It's not Carlos anymore. It's him. Rivas."

"Some of the runners say they have seen Carlos in town."

"It's just a front put on by Rivas to convince everyone that everything is business as usual. He'll spring his trap when they'll least expect it."

"I believe you, and so does Agent Wilcox, my contact in the North."

"Is he willing to work with us?"

"Yes. He wants to meet with you."

"When?"

"He's in town, so it's up to you. How soon can you be available?"

"I'm ready now."

"How about tomorrow morning in my office? Do you know how to get here?"

"I'll find you."

The wind had died down, but the rain continued to pound the city into submission. Nando planned on retrieving his car from Tokyo's garage as soon as the rain subsided. He offered to drive Xiomara to Spanich's office in the morning. If everything worked as planned, they would be done with that business by nightfall.

"You'll be safer here," said Nando.

"I'll go crazy if I stay cooped up here. Besides, I wouldn't want you worrying that I would run off so that I wouldn't have to pay you."

What she really meant was that despite his hospitality and general inclination toward helping them, Tokyo gave her the creeps.

"Suit yourself," said Nando, "although I'm not worried about that."

By the time they had reached the edge of the landfill, they were swabbed in slime from the knees down and soaked everywhere else. From the perimeter of the landfill, it was a two-block trek by foot to the nearest bus stop, where they boarded the downtown connection to the body shop where Nando had dropped off his car prior to the Chihuahua job. The once silver '78 Mercury Cougar looked like it had been sandblasted, doused with water, then run through a dust storm. The only items that had even a hint of aesthetic appeal were a set of shiny chrome rims. Only the passenger door worked, and the seats had been torn out, replaced with two iron stools.

"I guess there's no point in asking where the seat belt is," said Xiomara.

"This isn't a car," Nando said as he demonstrated some of his automobile's most impressive features such as the two-inch-thick plexiglass windshield, the shotgun clipped to the dashboard, and a trapdoor where the backseat had once been. "It's my partner in crime."

Despite the rain, the city was the usual snare of exhaust fumes, litter, and motorists who ignored traffic lights and mistook sidewalks for passing lanes. The streets were slowly turning into canals concealing huge chunks of missing asphalt that were more like craters than potholes. Still, it was all a welcome relief from the landfill. Even the smog smelled sweet in comparison.

"I could ask them to give you amnesty as well," said Xiomara as they rounded Avenida de las Américas, which led straight through the city toward the Chamizal Bridge and into El Paso.

"Why would you do that?"

"What would you do if I didn't?"

"Stay with Tokyo for a while in Villa Oscura, maybe move south to the provinces."

"The money is in El Paso. I thought you were going to stay with me until I paid you."

"I was hoping you would send it to me."

"As you wish."

The rain had intensified as they pulled into the parking lot of El Loro. Nando was secretly hoping that Mexicali Rose's conscience would sway her to let them stay for the night. Even if she hadn't been involved in the takedown back in Chihuahua, she was the one who had sent him on the job, despite his apprehensions. If not, maybe a percentage of his fee would convince her. The thought of going back to the landfill was not sitting too well with him at the moment. He had heard of people contracting mysterious, sometimes fatal, diseases by just breathing the putrid air.

"Wait here," he said, keeping the engine of the Cougar running and setting the timer on the small dashboard clock. "If I'm not out in twenty minutes, get out of here and find your way back to the landfill. Tokyo will make sure you get to the meeting."

"Just get back within twenty minutes, and we won't

have to worry about that."

A naked, bald-headed man with a black star-shaped tattoo under each bloodshot eye answered the door of the loft above the nightclub. He was woozy and reeked of marijuana. After sizing Nando up with heavy, half-shut eyes, he steadied his penis with one hand and began to take a leak at Nando's feet.

"I'm looking for Mexicali Rose," Nando demanded.

With his penis unsheathed and still dripping, the man slammed the door in Nando's face without another word. Nando looked down at the car and saw the small face of the girl looking up at him, a faint, hopeful smile curling her mouth. The wind was picking up again. As he turned to knock a second time, the door flung open, and the same dopey man stood before him, bidding him entry.

"I had a dream about you last night," said Rose, from amidst the folds of wrinkled bed sheets. She seemed even fatter without clothes. Someone was puking in the confines of the dark, smoky studio apartment. "I dreamed that you had been elected president."

"Surprised to see me?"

"Not really. I figured you'd be showing up here sometime. Too bad you missed the party last night."

A tall, lanky woman with red hair and breasts that had been tattooed so that the areolas looked like two huge eyeballs appeared at the doorway that led to the bathroom, wiping her mouth with her forearm. Mexicali Rose handed her a bottle of beer, which she downed in one feverish tilt. She then bent down onto the bed, buried her hands into Rose's furrows of flesh and tongue-kissed her. The bald-headed stoner giggled.

"I'm sorry, I don't have your cut of the transport money."

"Did you blow it all on those retarded Chihuahua whores?" The redhead had now worked her way down to Rose's mammoth breasts. "I know you'll find some way of settling your account."

The stoner had disappeared. Nando tried to remember if he had heard the door open, but was certain he had not, and there were no windows large enough for him to have crawled through. He listened for movement in the bathroom, but all that he could hear was driving rain and the smacking of the redhead's lips. His instincts alerted him that fifteen minutes had elapsed, and for a second he thought he had heard the sound of a car horn.

"I was going to ask if I could hang out at the club tonight, but I see that you don't need any more distractions," he said, mapping out in his head the quickest escape route toward downtown.

"Don't be silly," said Rose, brushing aside her lover and reaching for a cigarette. "We have plenty of room for you . . . and a guest. You can stay here in the loft."

Eighteen minutes had elapsed, and Xiomara had already slipped into the driver's seat. She decided to give him five more minutes. She lowered the fogged-up window on her side of the car and hoped the fresh air would calm her racing heart. She had been watching the traffic, the street corners and rooftops, looking for anything abnormal, but what did she know? Even after two years with Carlos, she had never been exposed to the inner workings of the world he dominated, into the intricacies of how the street was run and fought. But something inside her, some subliminal chime or road flare of the subconscious, was insisting that things were no longer okay, that Nando was in trouble, and that she was being watched. She honked the horn and held her breath.

Just as she leveled her hand over the gearshift, Nando burst through the loft door. He sprinted down the steps and motioned for her to gun the engine. Behind him a shirtless man with no hair was swinging a machete. She thrust the gearshift into reverse and stomped on the accelerator. The car roared and sprayed gravel as it shot toward the street. During the split second that it took her to shift into drive, Nando made it into the passenger seat, wailing in pain as he dragged his injured leg in.

"It's them!" he shouted.

They flew down the previously quiet boulevard. The bald man was right behind them in a tan-colored van. A series of gunshots rang out, but there was no way of telling if they had been fired by the pursuer or by some, as yet, unseen assailant. Nando had picked up the sawed-off shotgun and was feeding shells into it.

"Turn right!" he shouted as they approached the next intersection.

Another vehicle had joined the chase, this one screeching as it sped toward them from the oncoming lane. The Cougar slid across the flooded street as Xiomara threw the steering wheel hard to the right. The trailing cars nearly collided as they met at the intersection, but quickly managed to fall back into line to continue the chase. Several more shots rang out, and this time one of them struck the back window of the Cougar, shattering it into a web of intersecting cracks. Nando rammed it with the butt of the shotgun and cleared the ruptured glass. Then he fired at a black SUV that was not more than twenty feet behind them. The SUV swerved but only managed to evade part of the scattering load as half of its grille was blown away.

"Turn right," Nando shouted once again as they cleared the next intersection. Xiomara executed an almost perfect turn that sent both of the chasing vehicles barreling into each other as they each tried to mimic the Cougar's maneuver.

"God," gasped Xiomara as she slammed on the brakes.

Ahead of them two more black SUVs had sealed off

the street. A line of gunmen had taken positions in front of the vehicles, forming a human barricade that stretched from one sidewalk to the other. Peering into the rearview mirror, she discovered that the two pursuing vehicles had recovered and were creeping slowly up behind them.

"Move the car over that water," said Nando, setting down the shotgun. When the car had stopped, he unlatched the trap door. "Go," he said, nodding toward the oily pool that filled the massive pothole.

"Are you crazy?" she begged.

"It's the only way," he said. "You'll have to stay under the water while I distract them, hopefully lead them away from here. Get back to the dump. No matter what, don't miss your meeting with the reporter."

"What about you?"

"They would have gotten to me eventually. If you don't go, we're both dead."

Slowly she lowered herself into the freezing water, head first. The pothole was wide and deep enough to engulf her whole. She took a large breath and went under. Above her the trapdoor slammed shut, and seconds later she heard the howl of the Cougar as it raced toward the roadblock. There was a barrage of gunfire and the shudder of wrenching metal. Car engines snarled and tires screamed as the earth shook with the fury of a fresh chase. When she resurfaced for air almost a minute later, the street was quiet and empty except for the sound of the rain and the smell of burned rubber and gunpowder.

It was almost dark by the time she arrived at the dump, shivering, exhausted, and hungry. A cold can of soup in Tokyo's garage sounded like nothing short of paradise after a day of crouching in alleys, panicking at the sound of every approaching car, accosting strangers for directions to the dump, and wondering what had happened to Nando. She reserved a sliver of hope that he had escaped, but against so many of them it was implausible.

They had appeared out of nowhere, shooting with impunity. She knew Rivas well enough to know that it was now more than a matter of insuring that his coup would be successful. It was he against her, his pride against her defiance, his bloodthirsty rage against her will for deliverance.

Xiomara approached the garage with caution, waiting for Calvo to pounce, but there was no sign of the rabid Doberman. There was no answer when she knocked on the door, and she found that it was unlocked. She decided that she would rather face Calvo's wrath than another minute in the cold rain.

The room was dark but warm. Feeling her way around, she found the mattress that Nando had lain upon and collapsed into it. She screamed as her body struck something limp, wet, and furry. There was a click as the lights flicked on. The disemboweled remains of Tokyo's dog were strewn across the mattress. Her hands and the front of her blouse were smeared with his blood.

"The Baja-Cruz brothers want her alive," said a voice. She turned and saw two men aiming black pistols at her, their faces hidden behind wool hoods. One of them lowered his pistol and walked toward her, uncoiling a length of white rope. He clutched her by the throat and wrestled her to the ground. She tried to resist but was too weak to put up much of a fight. With the man's knees crushing her chest, she began to gasp for air. Squirming, she freed one of her hands. With her last ounce of strength, she fired her thumb upward and into her assailant's eyes, driving her fingernails into the gelatinous tissue of his irises.

Squealing, the man raised his hands to his eyes, crumbling to the floor where he covered his face in agony. Xiomara sucked in a mouthful of air and tried to roll away, but the other gunman was on top of her almost immediately. Pinning both of her arms with his knees to the floor, he began to strike her face and the sides of her head with unrelenting savagery. White light flashed each time a blow struck, and she could feel the blood seeping into her throat. The flurry continued as her cheekbones and nose shattered. Suddenly she heard someone scream, and the blows ceased. She opened her eyes and, through a reddish, blurry haze, saw a figure standing above her holding what looked like a large tree branch. She passed out before her eyes could focus enough to identify the apparition.

The first thing Xiomara sensed when she came to was the glorious warmth enveloping her body. The bliss only lasted until she tried to move. Her head felt like it weighed a ton, and her face was swollen numb. Every breath, every blink, every muscle quirk ignited a mushroom cloud of pain that seemed to disintegrate her whole body. All around her, jittery shadows danced on cavernous walls painted with the light from what at first seemed like a huge bonfire.

"She's awake," a woman's voice announced.

A face hovered over her. The man seemed familiar, but deciphering his facial characteristics was momentarily too much for her wrecked brain to execute. He placed a hand on her forehead and detonated another three-megaton explosion of pain. She wanted to cry but was discovering that her awareness, as limited as it was, was being over-whelmed by the sensory input, and she was slipping back into unconsciousness.

Xiomara was back home in her mother's kitchen eating freshly baked sweet bread, the kind her mother sprinkled with colored sugar. Pink was her favorite. Someone called her name. When she turned her head to look, a blast of wind struck her face and knocked her to the floor. When she looked up, she was sitting in the middle of an endless grass field. Her hands and feet throbbed with a dull pain. She looked down and saw hypodermic needles sticking into the back of her hands and her ankles. They were everywhere, thousands of them littered all around her in the grass. Every time she moved, one of them would puncture some part of her body. Soon there were needles clinging to her thighs, her forearms, her stomach and breasts, her neck, her face, back, and buttocks. She ran through the grass hoping to reach a haven where she could stop and remove the hideous needles, but the more she ran, the more the needles sank into her. Then her foot caught something and she crashed into the grass. There was a growl somewhere close by that grew louder and fiercer as she scurried along the ground. She came to a clearing where a dog that looked like Tokyo's Doberman confronted her. It was feasting on something that must have been particularly tasty by the sound of the dog's smacking snout; it was something that had been wrapped in a thin blanket, something attached to a long, pulsing cord. She followed the cord as it wound through the grass, twisted and tangled, and, to her horror, ran up the inside of her thigh. The dog looked up from its feast and bolted toward her. She was running again, her feet no longer touching the ground. She was falling into darkness. The plunge was brief as she landed with a shallow splash onto a pile of rotting corpses. They began to writhe, moaning and clawing at her face and body, sucking her under like quicksand until she was consumed by the mass of lique-fying flesh.

Xiomara could see again. Not well, but she could make out the details of her surroundings. She was in a tunnel about twenty feet high and twice as wide. A shallow stream of liquid flowed through the pockets of movement on each side of it. All along the walls of the tunnel, small tubes shot out thin, blue licks of flame that made the walls look like they had been decorated with Christmas lights. Close by, a child was crying.

"She wakes," said a voice.

A spike of pain impaled her spine when she tried to sit up, but she willed it away and was able to prop herself up on her elbows. One of the blue spears of flame glowed above her head. She could feel its warmth on her forehead. A man sat at her feet, scooping food from a metal can into his mouth with two fingers. Behind him a woman bounced a little girl in her lap. The little girl was crying, and one of her feet was covered with a black crust.

"They cut off her toe," said the man.

"Who?" croaked Xiomara.

"The same men who tried to kill you. They wanted to know where you were. They said they wouldn't stop cutting until we told them. My sister gave in after the first one. I'm sorry."

"Should have told them right away."

"They're not men. They're not even animals. They're demons, creatures that live off of fear and blood. You fed my family for three days. I did not want to betray you. But they would have killed her."

"How long have I been here?"

"Almost a week. We all have. They destroyed our homes and threatened to kill everyone if we didn't tell them where you and the injured man were. So we came down here into the tunnels to hide. Many of the dump dwellers prefer to live down here because it's warm and safer than on the surface. They even drilled the walls to siphon out the methane so they can light the fumes. I hate it down here. We are like rats waiting to get drowned."

The events of the past week were coming back to her in fragments. She recalled the shooting in the desert that had left Nando wounded and the dump and Tokyo and her escape through the trapdoor, a man beating her and saying something about the brothers wanting her alive. The Baja-Cruz brothers. Rivas would have forbidden his men from harming her in that manner. She knew he wanted her intact so that he could take her apart himself.

"Were those the same men who shot your friend?"

"I don't think so," she said.

"Then I pray for you."

Hoping to restore the equilibrium in her head, Xiomara drank some water and leaned into the wall of the tunnel. Her wounds were beginning to reawaken. The swelling in her nose partially blocked her vision. With her jaw crooked and her teeth loose, she had to tilt her head back so that the saliva would drain into her throat and not dribble onto her chin. It hurt to breathe. By virtue of some miracle, her tongue had escaped injury, and so it was with broken speech that she continued speaking to the man, whom she eventually recognized as the one who had led her to Tokyo's garage. Hearing his voice and responding to his questions was the only way she could keep the madness of the pain away. His sister fed her, even though most of the precious bowl of soup wound up on the front of her dress, and the little girl picked the dried blood from her hair.

There was no day or night, only an occasional report about the weather, the status of the dump, news about events in the city, from those who ventured to the surface periodically. The swelling in her face began to diminish as did the pain that had prevented her even from seeking a private place to relieve herself. The other figures inhabiting the shadows of the tunnel went from being disembodied echoes and fuzzy shapes to brisk outlines of men, women, and children, their faces dim yet unmistakable, their legs poised and durable, the hands purposeful, diligent. They had established a subterranean community where families cooked meals and washed clothes, where sorrow and hope intermingled, where new life was created and extinguished. Memories were relived, fears exchanged. Someone's sister had died back home. A father had returned from the North. There was talk of an upcoming nuptial. New members arrived and left every day, maintaining the fragile social balance of this quarter-mile length of sewer that had become the home of some fifty lost souls.

"I salvaged these from Tokyo's garage before the looters could get to them," the man said one day.

Xiomara examined the items in the plastic garbage bag he had dropped at her side, recognizing the laptop computer, the jogging suits, radios, cell phones, videocassettes, and a few soup cans. A smile came to her face as she remembered the first night she and Nando had spent there, when she had washed his body. She had been thinking a lot about him lately. A week had passed and with it the faint hope that perhaps he had escaped and would make his way back to the dump, or that someone would bring him to the tunnel.

"Some of it belonged to the two men who attacked you. One of them dropped this."

He handed her a chrome cigarette lighter with an eagle engraved into its side, and a black cellular phone, smaller than the three that Tokyo had owned. Shaking the lighter, she discovered that it was still nearly full. Then she tried the cell phones. They were all dead, except one of Tokyo's, but the battery was almost drained.

"Some of this stuff is valuable," she said. "You should try to pawn it."

"I don't know what half of this stuff is. Maybe you can tell me how much it's worth."

"Sure, whenever you want. But what did they do with Tokyo?"

"He was gone by the time I arrived. I wouldn't hold out too much hope for him. Strangers in expensive-looking vehicles with tinted windows have been making rounds every day, detaining anybody in sight, torturing and interrogating them before shooting them in the head. Someone overheard one of the dump dwellers talking about the tunnel, but the men thought he was crazy. Still, it's only a matter of time before they find the rest of us. This is the last place we have."

"What is your name?"

"Tomás."

"I'm Xiomara."

She looked around her at the world she had inadvertently become a part of. At first sight it was a hideous existence of darkness and misfortune. They were the wretched of the wretched, people unaccounted for by anyone, as insignificant to the whole of society as a nest of rats. Yet there was something pure about these people, something venerable about them, about the manner in which they suffered and adapted and survived. Theirs was an existence without pretense or greed or ambiguity. There was no corruption here, no misguided idealism, political sanctimony, or prescribed notions of morality. There was only life, death, and the countless triumphs and tragedies in between. And now even this was being taken away from them, and over what? A political game over control of something that made people forget who they were.

That night it rained in the outside world. The water poured into the earth and drove everyone to the uppermost edges of the tunnel so that by nightfall they were lined up against its walls, the few articles they considered valuable slung on their shoulders, hoping that the water would not rise any farther. Xiomara had retrieved the bag Tomás had brought from Tokyo's garage and raised it above her head to keep it out of the water that had now reached her ankles. The tunnel had become full with the desperate, pleading cries of men and women alike.

"We've got to get out of here now," she screamed to a bewildered Tomás, who was clasping his sister by the arm while trying to balance Melisa—the name they had given the little girl because she could not remember her original name. "Which way is the exit?"

"Over there," he said, pointing toward the direction

from which the water was coming. Then, without another word, he gathered his family and trudged into the middle of the current where the water reached past their knees. She followed right behind, as did the others when they realized what was about to occur and what had to be done.

Prayers were shouted toward the ceiling of the tunnel as the current rose to their waists and increased its force. The children were hoisted onto the shoulders of the adults, most of the items they had been carrying surrendered to the water by now. Behind them a roar like that of a speeding train shook the entire tunnel, and a fresh harvest of screams reverberated along the trembling walls. A massive current was fast approaching. They quickened their pace, churning their legs as fast as the water would allow.

The water began to recede momentarily as the tunnel sloped upward, yet by the time they had reached the iron bars that guarded the entrance hatch to the tunnel, it had reached their chests. It required the combined strength of three men to throw open the bars of the hatch that spilled out onto the surface of the dump. After helping to push Melisa onto the surface, Xiomara climbed up and began the arduous task of helping Tomás and the others pull the rest of the group from the tunnel and into the tempestuous night.

It was dawn by the time everyone who had survived had been pulled out. Two children had been swept away by the current. A woman had died of a heart attack, and another had suffered a miscarriage. The rain had slackened to a cold drizzle, and they all huddled en masse hoping for the coming day to bring with it the sun and new hope. Despite everything, there was a sense of accomplishment among the group, a feeling that they were still capable of something, however small it seemed.

"We can't stay here long," said Tomás. "The desert is our only chance."

"I will have you in my prayers," Xiomara said.

"You are safer with us," said Tomás, confronting her with the firm, logic-bearing stare of a father.

"But you are not safer with me," she said, raising a hand to his face.

Without further protest, he handed her one of the soup cans and a pen knife. She watched them file through the wet decay as they headed for the eastern edge of the city toward the desert that had delivered her and Nando what seemed like ages rather than days ago. Slowly, each of the dump dwellers disappeared into the gray mist of the sodden dawn. She felt hopelessly alone, forgotten, and lost. There was nowhere to run and nowhere to return to. Perhaps she, too, had now become one of them, a dump dweller.

Xiomara remembered what Marina had said about fate and the two destinies, the two prospective paths in life, one predetermined, the other left to be written by the individual. It didn't matter much to her at that point, but she was unwilling to allow her misfortunes to destroy anyone else's life. Often the silent were just as guilty as those who perpetrated pain and death. If they wanted her so badly, they would have her. It was time to end it. Digging into the plastic bag Tomás had brought to her, she retrieved the working cell phone. The battery icon was flashing. She would possibly have time for one phone call. Searching through the digital directory, she found a listing for Rose. It would be her one and only shot.

Mexicali Rose feigned ignorance when Xiomara revealed her identity. Still, her want for the information she was about to hear came through as thick and claustrophobic as the stench of the dump. The cell-phone battery died just as she told the woman there would be but one chance to nab the fugitive wife of Carlos Arquimedes-Savón.

The access hatch of the tunnel was located approximately fifty yards from Tokyo's garage, right beneath the biohazard signs. She thought about venturing back into the garage to look for a gun or a blanket—the mattress,

even with the dog's blood all over it, would be a blessing—
but time was running out.

The rain had tapered off by noon, and it was then that
she crawled back into the tunnel. The water level had subsided, but it was still high enough to make walking difficult. Wading through the water, she saw the remnants of
the camps that had contained life only hours earlier: dent-
ed pots, clothing, soiled toys. She marveled at their char-
coal drawings on the concrete walls. Then she saw the
body of one of the children who had drowned, lodged
between one of the vents in the wall. The little boy was
still holding the figurine of an action hero that was unrecognizable because the features of its head had been worn
away. His face was frozen in terror and disbelief. She freed
him, setting him afloat on the ebbing current that would
carry him to his final resting place.

It took her the rest of the day to extinguish the flam-
ing tubes. The choking methane began to fill the tunnel.
Farther past the ladder that led to the access hatch, she
found a vent large enough for her to crawl into and close
enough to the hatch to get some respite from the rising
concentration of the gas. It was here that she finally sat
down to eat the soup that Tomás had rationed to her,
puncturing holes in the can, one by one, with the pen
knife until enough of the lid was pried open to allow her
to drink the soup.

The methane drove her from the tunnel before dawn.
Xiomara waited by the access hatch, the plastic bag at her
side. She had discarded her soaked clothes and put on one
of Tokyo's jogging suits. It was light and soft and, best of
all, dry. After taking out the fancy lighter, the last thing
she would need, she dropped the bag through the access
tunnel into the watery depths below.

The landfill was peaceful, the morning beautiful. Sitting on a pile of metal drums marked with a skull and
crossbones and cellophane bags that contained a reddish

liquid with bits of gray matter floating in it, she primed her senses for anything signaling their arrival—the sound of a car engine, the smell of exhaust, the vibration of footsteps. The magnification of her awareness was uncomfortable. Every bird in the sky became an airplane or a helicopter ready to rain bullets on her. Every shadow was a potential sniper, and every surrounding garbage pile the trap from which her demise would spring.

Then she saw them, tiny black dots that emerged from behind the gates of the landfill that bordered the city limits. A caravan of five vehicles, a black Suburban guarded by two black jeeps, a white van, and a large maroon pickup adorned with a multitude of antennas and tires that looked like they belonged on a tractor rather than a passenger vehicle. They circled the perimeter of the landfill, looking for an avenue into the interior of the dump where she had told the woman the garage was located.

As the caravan turned into the road that led through the former encampment of the dump dwellers and cut into the center of the landfill en route to her present location, she climbed on top of a metal drum and raised her arms. The caravan disappeared behind a hill momentarily. When it reemerged, she could see the platoon of gunmen riding in the back of the giant pickup truck.

The vehicles came to a halt in front of the garage. The gunmen had already trained the scopes of their rifles on her. The passengers in the jeeps got out first, flashing their sunglasses and cocking their pistols. They did a quick sweep of the immediate area, then one of them sent a hand signal to the men in the pickup, who promptly jumped down and took up positions at various points around the landfill. Two of them climbed onto the roof of the white van and hoisted rocket launchers onto their shoulders. All of them remained motionless for minutes, frozen at their posts, ready to annihilate everything.

Then the door of the Suburban slid open, and another bevy of bodyguards, all of them in dark, elegant suits, emerged. They scanned the sky and sniffed the air before nodding toward the interior of the Suburban, where seconds later the small angular head that could have belonged to only one man appeared, aiming a pair of binoculars at her. A tall, muscular-looking man with blond hair followed as Rivas stepped out of the Suburban. Then they all fell into the defensive spearhead formation, with Rivas and his fair companion behind the point man and out of harm's way as they began walking toward her.

As they approached, Xiomara jumped off the metal drum and skirted over to the top of the tunnel access hatch. The smell of methane was so intense that it made her gag. She surveyed the landfill, hoping the others had taken the bait as well, but with Baja-Cruz it was impossible to tell. Her only consolation was that Rivas and his men had gotten this far. If Baja-Cruz wanted her as badly as Rivas did, they would come as well.

"Who could have thought that a little peasant girl could be so much trouble?" Rivas sneered as his men surrounded her.

"I'm tired of running," she said. "I want to come home."

"First of all, I think apologies are in order for Agent Wilcox. You missed the meeting the reporter had arranged with him."

The blond-headed man beamed a set of brilliantly white teeth at her, his cold gray eyes laughing. He opened his cell phone and whispered into it.

"I was scared," she said. "I thought you were going to kill me."

They all laughed, and she shrank in the glaring rays of the blooming daylight, cocking the lighter, feeling the warm methane fumes swirling around her.

"You know I would not have risked my own life to come here if I didn't want you to come back to me." Rivas stepped in front of her and began caressing her face. She winced as he touched the bruises and cuts. "Besides, I know it was the old man who put you up to this. He is out of the picture now. It's just you and me, and together we will rule this country."

Xiomara took a step back, keeping the lighter hidden in her palm. Just then, two more gunmen arrived, escorting three individuals. One of them was almost as fair-skinned as Agent Wilcox, but with brown hair. She didn't recognize him. A slouching Nando limped closely behind, followed by Tokyo, whose face was pocked with fresh glistening blisters.

"You must understand that before you can return, you have to prove your loyalty to the organization once again," Rivas said. He reached into his suit and produced his trademark 9-mm Beretta. "You can start by disposing of some garbage. We are, after all, in the most appropriate place for it."

"Let them go," she said, flicking the lighter and holding up the flame for all to see. A cadence of cocking firearms rippled through the air. "If I drop this lighter, the methane fumes beneath our feet will ignite and we all die. Let them go."

"Inventive," said Rivas, "but hardly credible. Spanich."

Agent Wilcox drew his pistol and fired a round into the brunette man's head, who remained upright momentarily, then doubled over and fell into the garbage. Xiomara turned and tossed the lighter into the access hatch, then dropped to the ground and constricted into a fetal position. She heard the lighter clank as it fell, then a shallow splash. Rivas began to laugh.

"I am not going to kill you," he said, wiping tears from his eyes. "After you shoot these two lice, I am going to cut off your arms and legs. I will remove your eyes, cut out your tongue, and singe your eardrums with acid. You'll spend the rest of your life in a cage eating the bread crumbs I will toss to you from time to time, shitting on yourself and satisfying the sexual appetites of every species with a will and a hard-on."

A sound like the roar of a jet engine filled the air around them. The earth began to shake violently, and before anyone had time to react, the ground began to cave in as huge plumes of flames shot toward the air. The access hatch had become a sinkhole spewing a thick geyser of fire.

The explosion had knocked all of them to the ground. The bodies of Tokyo and several of the gunmen had either been half-buried or were being consumed by the balls of flame that were rocketing up everywhere. There was no sign of Rivas or Nando. Agent Wilcox had landed a few feet from where she lay, and was crawling toward her, his manic grin in full bloom. She tried to scamper from his reach, but he was on his feet before she was. He tackled her to the ground and straddled her chest as he clutched her throat, holding his pistol to her temple. A shot rang out. Agent Wilcox's head exploded and spilled all over her. A helicopter zoomed by overhead, and gunfire erupted from every direction.

Baja-Cruz had arrived.

The entire landfill was on fire. The ground trembled and spat from the impact of the bullets. Tossing aside the large headless corpse of Agent Wilcox, she began to search the garbage heaps for Nando, who had been the farthest from the access hatch when it had exploded. The blast could have knocked him unconscious, in which case he would be relatively safe, stretched out on the ground if the fire hadn't gotten to him. It was also possible that he had fled mid the chaos, but she doubted it. In her heart she believed he would have come looking for her if he could. If the sinkhole had swallowed him, he was doomed.

Another helicopter joined the gun battle. It swooped in over the landfill firing a pair of missiles that rocked the ground again. She began calling his name, desperate now because time was running out. The moment either Rivas or the Baja-Cruz men spotted her, it would be game over. Crouching as low to the ground as possible, she headed for the garage, hoping that Rivas's gunmen had abandoned their posts and thinking that if she had to, she would make a run for it in one of the cars. She had almost cleared the garbage piles when a sharp, searing pain pierced her side. She turned as she fell and saw Rivas aiming his 9-mm at her.

Her heart began to race as she lay on the ground, bracing her mind for the last few moments of her life. Above her, one of the helicopters exploded as a ground-to-air missile tore through it. It splintered into a confetti shower of metal and glass that floated toward the ground, leaving a cloud of smoke where the explosion had occurred. Rivas appeared, kneeling beside her as he brought the gun up between her legs.

"The bullet will shoot up your cunt and blow out the top of your head," he said. "Best fuck you'll ever ha—."

He was cut off in midsentence by a thrusting side kick to the head. Nando rushed to him before he could recover and get off another shot, but he was too slow. Rivas caught him with an uppercut to the groin that brought him to his knees. Both of them remained on the ground, stunned by the blows they had exchanged. Finally, Rivas pulled his gun up and careened it toward Nando's face.

By now Xiomara had worked her way to her knees. In front of her, one of the bags of waste had ruptured, spilling a mass of dirty hypodermic needles. Grabbing one in each hand she charged Rivas, driving one of the needles into the side of his neck, the other down over his head, impaling his right eye. He squealed and fired a shot that nicked Nando in the ear. She stabbed out with two more needles, one puncturing his throat, the other his left eye.

Blinded, Rivas rose to his feet and commenced an

erratic almost comical march around the flames, wailing and clawing at the air. He eventually made his way toward the sinkhole. Sensing the danger, he stopped and turned. Xiomara straightened her body and made her way toward him. Her outstretched palms struck him flush in the chest, and he plunged headlong into the fiery pit. Dazed, bleeding, and out of breath, she stumbled back to where Nando lay and dropped down next to him as she tried to block the blood that was seeping from the bullet she had taken below the rib cage.

The call of sirens rose in the air as she laid her head on one of the plastic bags that were filled with the mysterious liquid and closed her eyes. With bullets still zipping by, flames raging, explosions thundering all around, and the sweet serenade of the sirens, she slipped into the most soothing and delicious sleep of her life.

Por ti, todo

Xiomara wasn't sure it was the right place, but how many combination cantina/*taquerías* could there be in a town that technically didn't even exist? The suitcase was surprisingly heavy, but she had insisted to Spider that she would carry it, even if it didn't turn out to be the place. She hammered the bell on the counter, but nobody came, so she and Spider walked behind the small shack, where they found a man sitting in a wheelchair next to a large black-and-red Harley Davidson motorcycle, his face dancing with the stiff, tepid offshore breeze. His fingers were curled into claws that were no good for wiping the curd of drool that had collected at the corner of his mouth.

"Nando Flores," she said.

The man said nothing and continued to caress the breeze with his cheeks.

"I'm here to see Nando Flores."

This time the man began to laugh, or it seemed to be a laugh, sounding more like the sound an excited pig would make. He raised a crooked arm and pointed toward the ocean. She could make out the outline of a sailboat, but no sign of anyone, except for a child, a girl playing in the sand. Leaving the man to his oblivion and his courtship with the wind, they walked toward the boat.

Nando had seen the two figures approaching. He recognized the woman, but not the man. Her father? An uncle, perhaps? A lover? No, he looked too old. He had heard that she was alive days after the police had released him, but his efforts at locating her had proved fruitless. He figured she had crossed over to the place he would never set foot on, not even for her. He could smell her, even at that distance, but he wouldn't look up. He would just continue to apply the new layer of paint to his only true love.

"I was beginning to think you didn't want to be found," Xiomara said.

"I didn't," Nando replied, spilling the paint.

"Nando, look, a mermaid," the girl shouted in the distance as she pointed to the sand.

"I'd like you to meet an old acquaintance," she said, turning to her companion. "This is Nando Flores, famous car smuggler of Ciudad Juárez and the man who saved my life. This is my security specialist, Spider."

The man bowed slightly but said nothing. His crisp suit flapped in the wind.

"I think you overexaggerate. By my account, we are even."

"Now we are," she said, lowering the suitcase to the sand.

"You should give that to someone who really needs it, those people back at the dump."

"They've been taken care of. Business is rather slow in this part of the world, I hear."

"I get by."

"The organization could use a man with your expertise."

"The organization?"

"I meant . . . me . . . we . . . well, I was hoping that we could . . . when the time is right."

"I left all that behind."

"All of it?"

"Most of it."

"I see."

"Now, if you ever need a boat ride to Australia, I'm your man."

She smiled.

Acknowledgments

It is with sincere appreciation that I acknowledge the patience and support of Dr. Ben L. Parker, Dr. Marvin Cox, and Dr. Mary Rohlfing. Special thanks to Raul Muñoz for his insight and Trent Young for his constructive criticism. I also wish to acknowledge the dedication and courage of those authors whose works inspired the composition of *Narco*. Many of them literally risked their lives in their quest for truth. Finally, I would like to thank my family, especially Veva, Iván and Isabel, for their undying love.